Douglings Adventures: BOOK 1

MYSTIC INFORMANT

Carissa Douglas

AUTHOR & ILLUSTRATOR

Scepter

COPYRIGHT © 2019 Carissa Douglas

The total or partial reproduction of this book is not permitted, nor its informatic treatment, or the transmission of any form or by any means, either electronic, mechanic, photocopy or other methods, without the prior written permission of the publisher.

PUBLISHED BY
Scepter Publishers, Inc.
info@scepterpublishers.org
www.scepterpublishers.org
800-322-8773
New York

All rights reserved.

TEXT AND COVER BY
Alston Taggart and Kevin Sample at Studio Red Design

Library of Congress Control Number: 2019947415

ISBN
Paperback: 9781594173639
eBook: 9781594173646

Printed in the United States of America.

MYSTIC INFORMANT

FOR MY AWESOME GODCHILDREN

Kaitlyn

Gage

Catherine

Nathaniel

Asha

Gemma

Justyne-Therese

Jonathan

and Jacob

MYSTIC INFORMANT

CHAPTER 1

A CHUBBY TODDLER WAS CLIMBING ALL OVER her: a foot digging into her belly, a hand grasping her poor, defenseless ear. Mary would normally have shoved her away, but her little sister, Kiara, was particularly cute that day dressed up as a flying unicorn. Kiara's dark hair was a mass of tangles swept into the hooded costume, and her light blue eyes shone with excitement.

"I being *pegahorn!*" she exclaimed. Mary laughed. She was no stranger to being bombarded by little kids. There were eleven children in the Douglas family, and the youngest five of the batch included: the troublesome two-year-old who was climbing on her; her three-year-old brother, Joachim; a set of one-year-old twins, James and Jacinta; and their baby sister, Callista. It was a little like living in a petting zoo, except a whole lot crazier and with lots of strange smells!

"Kiara threw Emma in the toilet!" Mary's older sister, Allora, stood with a stern look on her face, hands on hips and eyes glaring at the "pegahorn."

"Eeeewwww!" a tiny voice exclaimed, sounding more like a siren. It was little Jacinta (and that was her favorite word). Kiara buried her face in Mary's shoulder.

"What?!" Mary pushed the two-year-old away. "That's my dog!"

Kiara's eyes widened with the realization that she had lost her ally.

"No, it's actually mine!" Allora insisted. "And now she'll need a bath!" she huffed. "I'll have to throw her into the washing machine."

Mary frowned, "Poodles don't like washing machines. Her fur will never be the same!"

"Well, it's better than cuddling a stuffed animal that smells like toilet water," Allora retorted.

"Good point." Mary conceded. "Kiara, you're not supposed to touch our stuff or throw things in the toilet! You're not even potty-trained yet, so you have no business being in our bathroom at all!"

"We need to call a LCAMAS meeting pronto! We'll discuss this matter, as well as something else that requires our immediate attention." Allora always used big words when she was trying to sound official. "I'll round everyone up and we'll rendezvous in the clubhouse in five!"

"Rendezvous?" asked Mary.

"Meet up," Allora clarified, "in five!"

"Oh. Days?" asked Mary.

Allora sighed impatiently. "Minutes!!!"

LCAMAS (pronounced Luh-KAM-iss) was their secret club name. It was the acronym for the names of the oldest six kids in the family. Liam, who was thirteen; Christian, twelve; Allora, eleven; Mary, nine; Angelica, seven (and a half); and Serena, who was six. It was a way for them to discuss important older-kid business without the interruptions from the "Littles," which is what they called the younger Douglas kids.

Allora cut up six scraps of paper, scribbled "LCAMAS" on each piece, and then delivered them to the club members. Liam was reading a comic book in his bedroom when his paper arrived. Allora dropped it right on Superman's head.

"Hey!" Liam objected. But when he realized it was the LCAMAS calling card, he threw his book on the bed and headed to the clubhouse.

PING! Christian's message bounced off his head as he struggled to pry his lightsaber out of his brother, Joachim's, death grip. "Why are you throwing things at me?" he asked.

"Leave the lightsaber," Allora said. "We have more important things to deal with."

Christian released his grip and sent Joachim flying back onto the floor.

"NO FAIR!" Joachim cried. But when he realized he had secured his prize, he jumped up quickly and began waving the lightsaber in the air, singing: "MINE, MINE, ALL MINE!"

Serena and Angelica were playing with their Barbie dolls. All of a sudden, a red-headed Barbie bobbed toward their dolls, carrying two pieces of paper, one wedged under each of her plastic arms.

"Excuse me ladies," the Barbie squeaked, courtesy of Allora's best high-pitched voice. "Special delivery!" The girls giggled, but when they realized it was a call to a secret club meeting, they put on serious faces and scrambled outside.

The clubhouse was hidden among a batch of trees behind their home. Their backyard was a vast piece of land, with a small forested area and a winding river. The clubhouse sat on four large posts above a huge sandbox. The six older Douglas kids climbed up the ladder one by one and sat around a large table made from an old door and four cement blocks.

"Order!" said Allora in her most authoritative voice.

"I should be the one to call us to order!" insisted Liam. "After all, I'm the oldest."

Allora heaved a sigh. "You don't even know why I've called this meeting."

"Is it because Kiara threw Emma in the toilet?" Mary asked.

"That's one item we should discuss," replied Allora, "but there's more... I found something."

She reached deep into her pocket and produced a strange, ornate object.

"What is that?" Christian asked, lurching forward to get a better view. He was always the most curious of the bunch, and the loudest and, possibly, the pushiest.

"I'm not quite sure," Allora replied. "It almost looks like a sort of miniature sculpture or something."

Liam held out his hand. "Let me see it."

Allora readily handed the object over to Liam. He was a pretty smart boy. He learned to read when he was only three years old and was currently two school grades ahead. If anyone could figure it out, he could. Liam adjusted his glasses, as he always did when getting ready to analyze something of curious origin. The other children looked on with anticipation. You could almost see Liam's encyclopedic brain filtering through the endless files of his memory.

"I can't detect any evidence of its age or origin, but I can say with great certainty that it is not simply a sculpture. It's a key."

"Weird!" cried out Angelica. "Allora, where did you find it?"

Allora's eyes widened. "You probably won't believe me, but I think I was led to it."

"Okay, that makes it even weirder," Angelica said. "What do you mean?"

"I was praying at the grotto. When a thought was... how can I describe it? Almost *put* into my head."

The grotto was at the foot of their property near the river. Their mother and father had built it using large stones speckled with flecks of shiny silver. They had created the shell-like structure to house a beautiful, white statue of Our Lady of Fatima that stood almost two feet tall. There were beds of flowers on either side of the statue, and the ground in front was covered with grey slabs of flagstone. Their father had built a small bench off to one side, and the children loved to sit and pray and think about all sorts of things in that pretty little place.

"I was sitting on the bench and I *felt* words in my head. They were: *You are so close. Take off your sandals and dig by the heart-shaped pebble.* So I bent over to undo my sandals, and I saw it! The heart-shaped pebble! It was behind my foot, under the bench on a small mound of sand."

"This just can't get any weirder," Angelica said, her eyes round and filled with wonder. "Soooo, you dug and you found the strange key?"

"Yes," said Allora solemnly. "It was down pretty deep, and it was really dirty. I tried to wash away bits of hardened clay in the bathroom (that's when I found Emma in the toilet, by the way). I can't help but think it has a special purpose. Why else would I have been led to it?"

"We have to figure out what it's for," Mary asserted, "and who put it there and why, and what this all means, and ugghhhh! I can't take it." Mary was always prone to being dramatic, and this was just the type of excitement she needed to warrant a display of theatrics. She pressed the back of her hand to her forehead and pretended to faint from the magnitude of the questions at hand, but her foot caught the edge of one of the cement blocks holding up the table and she unwittingly fell onto her six-year-old sister.

"OFF!!!" Serena exclaimed. She shoved Mary with all her

strength, which was significant for someone of her short stature, and sent Mary rolling on top of the old door table. The makeshift table could not take the weight of its unexpected guest and snapped at the center. It caved in, and the four cement blocks all toppled with it. The children's shocked expressions soon gave way to fear, as they heard the sound of the boards under the wreckage creaking, almost groaning, and then slowly snapping.

Amid the children's shrieks, a mass of the floor of the clubhouse gave out and plummeted down into the sandbox below. The children were swimming in a cloud of sand and splints of wood.

Once the dust had settled, Christian called out, "Is everyone okay?" He was coughing and sputtering and had banged his shoulder on the frame of the sandbox, but he tried hard to compose himself.

The fall was only about six feet down and the rest of the structure had remained intact, but everyone was shaken from the experience. Mary was half buried in the sand and half on top of Serena, who yelled out, once again, "OFF!"

Allora was dangling from the edge of the clubhouse. "A little help, please!"

Liam was planted in the sand. He squinted his eyes as his hands frantically felt around the grit and splints of wood in search of his glasses. Finally, the tip of his finger grazed the familiar smoothness of lenses. He happily set them back in place and jumped up to rescue Allora.

"Thank you," she said, fully grateful as he carried her down to safety. Angelica looked accusingly at Mary, her lips tight and her brow furrowed, "Are you going to pretend to faint again? Because if you don't, I think I might, but FOR REAL!!!"

Christian stepped out of the pile of debris and surveyed the damage. He shook his head and sighed, "We are in so much trouble."

CHAPTER 2

THE NEXT MORNING THE LCAMAS MEMBERS trudged toward the clubhouse wearing work gloves, carrying shovels, and pushing a wheelbarrow. Their dad hadn't been as angry as expected. He'd inspected the remnants of the flooring and made sure that the rest of the structure was secure. Aside from a few scrapes and bruises, no one was seriously injured and so all were deemed fit to work. And work they did.

"This is going to take forever to clean up!" Serena complained.

Allora patiently explained, "We just have to take the broken wood to the burn pile and clear the debris out of the sandbox. It's not so bad. Besides, there are so many of us, we'll probably be done in no time!" In spite of the previous day's calamity, she was in a good mood. She held the key in her pocket and couldn't help smiling from the mystery and excitement of it all.

The children worked hard, pulling the worn slabs of wood from the sandbox and wheeling them away. Within an hour they were hauling out the last of the debris.

Then they saw it.

It was Angelica who first noticed the shiny object. One of the cement blocks must have fallen directly on the frame of the sandbox, cracking it open. The wood beam had split in two, exposing what looked like a metal panel underneath. "I need some help over here!" she called out. "There's something under this section of the sandbox. Can we rip out this part of the frame?"

"I don't know," Liam said cautiously. "If we pull that beam away, we'll lose a lot of the sand." He adjusted his glasses. "The sand is extra dry, from the lack of precipitation in the past two weeks. Its consistency will mean that it will readily pour out without a barrier to prohibit the flow."

"NOOOOOO!" The wail of their three-year-old brother was unmistakable. "DON'T SPILL MY SAND!"

Joachim ran toward them, arms flailing, his bright blue eyes wide with panic and his face red with alarm. Angelica's eyes were wide too. "I'm impressed that he understood anything you just said."

"It's fine, Joa," Mary assured the little boy. "Go back to the house."

"No, I love my sandbox," he insisted. "I don't want you to spill it."

"For goodness sake!" exclaimed Angelica, hands on her hips. She was small, but no one could match her feistiness and tenacity. "Someone help me pull away the beam!" Christian jumped at the chance to assist. His curiosity was tingling. Liam sometimes referred to it as his *spidey sense*.

The two children struggled to pull the two pieces of the beam away but realized the task was a bit too much.

"Come on guys!" Angelica ordered. "We need your help!"

Her determination was contagious, and soon all of the older children were pulling at the beam; even Joachim tried to help. They heaved together and with one last strong tug, the siblings fell back, toppling over one another as the two halves gave way. The sand poured out, revealing that the shiny metal panel extended all the way under a large portion of the sandbox.

"You spilled my sand!!!" Joachim cried out.

"SHHHH!" Serena hushed him. «Look!»

"What is that?!" Mary exclaimed. "It has some kind of strange writing on it."

The children cleared away the remnants of dirt that covered the surface of the metal. After clearing it off as best they could, they saw that it was actually not one but two large panels. They looked like two great doors laid out on the ground.

"Do you think it's some sort of bomb or tornado shelter?" Allora inquired. "Why would someone build a sandbox on top of a shelter?"

Liam shifted his glasses and leaned close to the panels. "I don't think this is a shelter at all. Look at these markings!"

The doors appeared thick and heavy. They were ornate, covered with strange symbols and etchings of thorns, crosses, and what looked like pieces of medieval armor. There were letters that were hard to make out.

"Is that French?" Mary asked. "It's definitely not English."

"I think it's Latin," Liam said. "I'll try to translate it, but it's a little hard to piece together. A few of the words are corroded and no longer decipherable." Liam had been studying Latin for the past three years and was actually becoming quite proficient.

"I can't make out the first word, but some of the words that follow are... " Liam cleared his throat and spoke slowly, «*Intraveritis... pro gloria Dei.*»

"Well, what does that mean?" Christian couldn't take the suspense.

Liam replied, "I think it means: *Enter for the glory of God.*"

"AMAZING!" Angelica cried. "We should definitely enter. It's for the *glory of God*, after all."

"But not all of the words are clear. What if there's more to it?" Allora submitted. "I don't know if I'm okay with this."

"WHAT?! You're throwing away the chance to unravel a mystery, to enter the unknown, to go on a once in a lifetime adventure!" Mary was back to her dramatic self again.

Allora frowned. "I'm just not sure."

Meanwhile, Christian had been trying to pry the doors open, but his efforts were in vain. He grabbed one of the shovels and wedged it between the two panels, hoping to use it as a lever. Using the full weight of his body, he pulled back. The wooden pole snapped at the shovel's neck.

"Oh man!" he cried out in frustration. "I don't think we can enter '*for the glory of God*' or for any other reason, 'cause these doors aren't budging!" The rest of the children tried to help Christian with the seemingly impossible task but were left feeling tired and highly disappointed. Only Allora seemed a little relieved.

Joachim sat merrily on one of the doors. "Here's some of my sand," he said to himself, smiling and digging out the sediment from a small hole in the panel.

"JOA!" Mary exclaimed. "You're a GENIUS!"

The chubby toddler smiled, "I know."

"No, I don't think you do. You just found a keyhole!" Her cheeks were flushed with excitement. "And it just so happens that we have a very special key!"

Allora took a few steps back. She put her hand in her pocket and began to nervously massage the coveted item. "I told you that I'm not sure about this yet," she stammered. "I think we need more information."

"Where are we going to get information on something as mysterious as this? I don't think anyone even knows it exists."

Christian couldn't stand the idea of being so close to solving the riddle of the key, yet prevented from taking another step forward. "You said you were led to the key, remember? You were meant to find it! Why, if not to open these doors?"

Allora tentatively pulled the key out of her pocket and stared at it, willing it to somehow reveal its purpose to her. "But... we don't even know if the key will work," she insisted. "We don't know enough about it; we should... "

"I can't take this!" Angelica blurted out. She grabbed the key from Allora's palm and ran over to the doors, forcing it into the small hole. It took a moment for Allora to recover from the shock of her sister's speed and gumption.

She called out, "Angelica, NOOOO!"

But it was too late. As Angelica turned the key, what looked like a small burst of lightning shot through the hole and she and Joachim were pitched backward onto the grass. The doors glowed and almost seemed to throb. With a loud *CRACK*, they separated and dropped open to a cavern below. The remaining sand flowed down through the opening, a fine powdery waterfall. Everyone froze except for little Joachim, who ventured to the edge of the doors and wailed. "NOW YOU SPILLED ALL MY SAND!"

"GET BACK, JOA!" Serena called out. She was very protective of her little brother. Joachim started to turn around, but his foot slipped on a small patch of sand, and in one wispy, slick motion, he disappeared into the dark void below.

CHAPTER 3

EVERYONE CRIED OUT AT ONCE AND RAN TO the opening. They dropped to their knees, calling out Joachim's name. But there was no answer. Not even a sound. The children would have preferred to hear the familiar wailing or whining that the toddler often produced when he hurt himself than to face the deafening silence that summoned the image of a boy too injured to speak... or worse.

"I'm going after him," Christian said with fierce determination.

"But we don't know what's down there," Serena said solemnly through her tears. "I'm scared."

Liam took his sister's hands and spoke softly to her. "We know our brother's down there."

Serena nodded slowly and said, "That's true." She wiped

her eyes and tried to muster her courage. "So I guess it doesn't matter what else we might find."

The siblings looked at one another, knowing what needed to be done.

They peered over the edge of the cavern. It was deep and dark, and it emitted a strange, musty smell.

Mary wrinkled her nose. "I don't like this," she stated.

Angelica hung her head down into the entrance to get a closer look. When she popped back up, she looked worried. "It's really deep. I don't know how we're going to get down there. Maybe we could try getting some rope to tie to one of the clubhouse posts or something."

"Wait! What's that?" Liam asked, pointing to a large, gold lever just inside the corner of the opening.

"I'm going to pull it!" Christian shouted.

"Wait!" Allora cried. She was fed up with everyone acting so impulsively. But it was too late. Christian shifted the lever and waited. Nothing happened.

"Well that was disappointing," he said.

Just then, the ground started to vibrate and a loud series of clicks penetrated their ears, followed by a thunderous rumble. They looked on with anticipation as stone planks shot out from a side wall one by one until they had created an archaic-looking flight of stairs.

"Awesome!" Christian said excitedly, "Let's go."

"Just let me grab some flashlights; otherwise we won't be able to see anything, let alone find Joachim," Allora said. She ran off to the garage and was back in a few minutes with three flashlights. Everyone wanted to carry one, but after a session of "Rock, Paper, Scissors," the bearers were Liam, Mary, and Serena—although Serena's flashlight was soon confiscated, as she kept saying, "Watch this!" and sticking it in her mouth, causing her cheeks to glow.

The six children slowly descended the staircase. There were cobwebs lining the stone walls, and the echo of their footsteps was carried far beyond the scope of the thin beams extending from their flashlights. The children felt as though they had been swallowed down a giant throat. Serena reached for Christian's hand. He took it gladly, in an effort to appear strong and confident. Although he would never have admitted it, he was drawing just as much comfort from the gesture. The staircase spiraled down, down, down until finally the children came to a dirt landing.

"This way," said Liam, "I think." He motioned toward the winding path ahead. It looked like an ancient tunnel with arched stone ceilings. Mary turned her head back toward the staircase. A stream of bluish light shot down from the opening above. It was a small comfort and she was reluctant to leave it behind, her last connection to the familiar world above. But she thought of her little brother and so ventured into the dark tunnel.

"This is taking a long time," Serena whispered. "I think I need to use the bathroom."

"No, you don't," Allora whispered back. "You're just nervous. We all are."

"I'm not," Christian asserted. No one really believed him, but they were still comforted by his attempt to appear brave.

They continued through the tunnel for what seemed like an eternity, and then they heard something strange and altogether unexpected.

Laughter. It was faint, but unmistakable, and what made it beautiful was that it was familiar. So familiar.

"JOA!!!" Angelica joyfully belted out. Soon everyone was calling his name and running, their voices echoing through the tunnel. They saw a warm light ahead and, as they turned a sharp corner, they found a large wooden door that was slightly ajar. They stopped as they heard something alarming.

It was a second voice.

One that was was deep, full, and strange.

"Wait!" Allora's voice was an urgent whisper, "We can't just run in there. We don't know who has him. We don't know what we're up against." She moved toward the door and peeked through the open crack. She saw two figures. One was the short, chubby silhouette of her little brother; the other was a man dressed in a long brown robe.

"You should come in," the gruff voice called out. "I think this little one would be delighted to be reunited with his family."

Mary gasped. "He knows we're here!"

"Of course he knows we're here," said Liam. "We were all just screaming Joachim's name a minute ago. Let's go."

With great labor, Allora pushed the large door. It was heavy and groaned as it opened to reveal the three-year-old standing, cheerfully grasping the hand of a man who appeared to be a type of monk. They were standing in front of a stone fireplace. The flames, warm and brilliant, chased the damp chill from the air and made the cave-like room feel cozy and less foreboding. Joachim grinned and exclaimed, "I found a JEDI MASTER!"

He turned to the old man and asked, "Are you Old Obi-Wan Kenobi?"

The old man looked quite confused. Joachim turned back to his siblings. "He's Old Obi-Wan Kenobi."

"No, he's not," Liam said, "but I think I know who he is. How is this possible?" Liam's face was a vision of awe and shock.

"Wait a minute!" Allora cried out. "I know who you are too! You're Padre Pio! You're a saint! You... you can't be here... you're um... " She didn't know quite how to say it. "Well... you're dead."

The old man chuckled. "Saints are not dead. You know that. In fact, I would argue that the heavenly saints are more *alive* than you are."

"But your body is incorrupt! I saw a picture of it online. This doesn't make any sense." Liam looked completely puzzled.

The man smiled and said, "If you knew me, then you'd know that I've never had trouble being in two places at once." He laughed to himself. It was true. The children had read stories about the life of St. Pio and his ability to do something miraculous called *bilocating*. He could be physically present in two places at once. There were many witnesses to this miracle.

"In this case," he continued, "I am here simply because Our Lord has called me to be thus. There is something you are being called to do, and God, in his great love for you, has called upon me to assist."

Angelica couldn't contain herself. "This is amazing! You can talk to angels too, right? Can you ask my guardian angel why he didn't catch me when I fell off my bike last week? I was really annoyed by that!"

Padre Pio was quiet, shaking his head and smiling, as though some hidden informant was filling his ears with a series of mischievous tales. "Your poor angel has been grossly overused. As to the incident you are referring to, he says he was kept busy helping to break the fall of the two-year-old you had propped on the handlebars."

Angelica's eyes widened with shock. "Oooooh yeah." She stepped back, wincing. "I hope he doesn't tell you anything else."

Padre Pio let out a hearty laugh. "Speaking of our dear friends, the guardian angels," he said, "your brother's angel was very hard at work today and, with the help of a very large pile of sand at the bottom of the cavern, he was able to keep your brother from the injury he should have received from the fall. Joachim here has been telling me all about your family. I've only been able to decipher about half of what he's been saying, but am I to understand that there are eleven children in your family? How ever does your mother keep all your names straight?!"

"There *are* eleven of us!" Mary said cheerfully, "But we're all pretty different. Liam is the oldest. He's the one over there with the blond wavy hair, blue eyes, and glasses. Christian's next. He's the one with brown hair and brown eyes. Allora is the one with the light brown hair, blue eyes, and glasses."

Allora waved shyly. Mary continued, "I'm next. I'm Mary and as you can see, I have brown hair and beautiful, hazel eyes."

"Ah, I see," the saint interrupted with a laugh, "and you must be the *humble* one." Mary gave a sheepish grin, and then happily continued. "Angelica is the one over there by the door with the long, wavy, golden hair and blue eyes, and Serena's the little one beside her with the blue eyes and super-long, super-straight, blonde hair. Of course, you already know Joachim. The youngest four aren't here. They're back at our house with our mom and dad."

Padre Pio smiled. "I shall require an inordinate amount of wisdom to remember all your names."

His eyes twinkled. "But I should very much like to get to know all of you."

"You said that God is calling us to do something," Allora said, as she timidly approached the saint. "Can you tell us what that is?"

The old man took a deep breath and said, "I'm not sure you're quite ready to hear it."

"We are!" yelled Angelica, "Just tell us!"

Padre Pio smiled and said, "Go now. Your mother's waiting for you. During your family Rosary this evening, pray that God will prepare you for what lies ahead. Tell no one about our encounter and meet me here tomorrow, except for you, little one." He bent down and planted a kiss on Joachim's tousled blonde hair. "You need to stay home and keep an eye on your younger siblings."

Joachim beamed and said, "I'll miss you, Obi-Wan. You

smell nice!"

The children promised to return the following day. As they filed out the door, Joachim turned and waved one last time to his new friend. "Bye, bye," he said. "Oh, and I'm gonna ask Mommy to send you some new gloves. Your gloves have all the fingers missing!"

The other children giggled. During his life on earth, Padre Pio had been known to wear partial gloves to cover his special gift called the *stigmata*, which allowed him to bear the wounds of Christ on his hands and feet. The saint called out, "You are a good boy! If you are ever in need, just send me your guardian angel."

CHAPTER 4

THE NEXT MORNING, THE OLDER CHILDREN IN the family rushed through breakfast. Their mother walked into the kitchen and witnessed the flurry of cereal flakes, the clanking of spoons, and the bottom of bowls as the children drank up the last of their milk with vigorous slurping noises.

"Um," she started. "What's going on here?"

The children all froze, uncertain of what to say.

"We're in a hurry to go outside," Allora said truthfully. "We really are!"

"Okay... " their mother said, "but I think you should pace yourselves. There's really no rush."

But there was. The children had barely been able to sleep the night before with all of the excitement of the previous day.

They couldn't wait to see their new friend again and perhaps learn the details of the special task that lay ahead.

They ran to the base of the clubhouse. They had closed the doors the evening before and had used some branches to cover them. Allora produced the special key and placed it excitedly into the lock. It wasn't nearly as dramatic this time; the doors simply fell open and the children descended the staircase once again.

"So you've returned!" the saint greeted them. "Wonderful. Now we can begin."

"What exactly does God want us to do?" Liam inquired.

Padre Pio took a deep breath. "It is not a task for the faint of heart."

"We're very brave," Christian said, placing his hands on his hips and puffing out his chest.

The saint chuckled, "I'm sure you are!" He grew serious. "But what you will encounter will require more than bravery. Your strength, perseverance, intelligence, and faith will be tested. You will be tried as you have never been. You will find it hard to go on, and at times, you will wish that you had never entered through the doors leading into this holy cavern."

Serena let out a gasp.

"Fear not, Little One. You will be given special gifts and supernatural graces to help you on this journey, and you will never be alone."

"Will you be with us?" Mary asked in earnest.

"Indeed," he said, "it is why I've been brought here; to assist you with your task. But I will not always be with you."

He continued, "Tomorrow you will be visited by a woman. She will appear to be all goodness, but she is not to be trusted. She has begun to weave a web that will ensnare your family with the intention of bringing about your ultimate ruin. She is aware of all the light that lives within your hearts and does not want that light to spread. She cannot be defeated by natural means, for she is not what she seems."

"That's terrible!" Angelica cried out. "When I see her, I'm gonna push her away and then call the police."

"No child," the saint said gently, "that will not do. As I said, she will not be defeated in that manner. In this first stage, you will especially need to clothe yourselves in kindness, selflessness, and humility."

"Um," Liam interjected, "that doesn't seem like a very strong defense."

"It is more powerful than you could ever imagine."

"I don't want to do this." Allora's voice was almost a whisper. As Padre Pio turned to meet her solemn gaze, her lip stiffened. "I didn't ask for this. I didn't agree to it and I'm certainly not ready to face these... huge trials... this woman. She sounds horrible, *EVIL* really. I'm not going to do it."

The saint's eyes were filled with compassion. "I understand your reservations. It is a heavy task, but you agreed to it when you turned the key and entered through the doors.

Did you not intend to heed the words inscribed?"

"The words were: *Intraveritis pro Gloria Dei*. That means: *Enter for the Glory of God!*" Liam insisted. "Or at least, those were the words we could make out."

Padre Pio shook his head slowly and said, "The phrase in it's entirety reads: *Ne intraveritis sed pro Gloria Dei*. Which translates to: *Do not enter but for the glory of God*. It means that no one should come through those doors unless they are willing to do the will of the Father and to bring him glory, no matter what that may entail. Entering through those doors has brought you into what would be best described as *a marrying* of the spiritual and physical worlds."

"Like a split dimension?" Christian asked excitedly.

Padre Pio smiled and shook his head. "I'm not familiar with that particular term, but what I mean to say is that in this place, you will encounter that which is entirely real at all times but is usually kept hidden from the sight and senses of man. You will be called to venture more deeply into that reality, going places most cannot go: seeing and doing things that few would ever believe, save through faith. There are those who have been pulled into this realm in offering themselves to darkness, but you, *you* entered through these blessed doors *for the glory of God,* and in doing so, you entered into an agreement, so to speak."

"We didn't know any of that," Allora exclaimed, "We didn't understand, and we also didn't have a choice because our brother had fallen in and we needed to find him."

The saint nodded and then he gazed intensely toward an

area just over their heads. He seemed to be in a sort of daze, listening and then humming as though pondering a notion that was being presented.

"I agree, Dear Friend," he spoke soundly, still staring above their heads. He then turned his attention back to the children. "My dear messenger has informed me that Our Lord does not intend to hold you to the words inscribed on the entrance. He recognizes that you acted with great love and courage in desiring to rescue your brother, that you did not understand the inscription, and he would never force you to do his will. You are not slaves to him but have been offered the choice to accept this task and bring him glory, or to walk away."

"We'll do it." It was a tiny voice, and all the children were shocked when they turned around and discovered its source: the smallest among them. Serena looked determined. "Guys, it's what God wants from us. And isn't God's will supposed to be perfect? And doesn't he love us more than anything? If we believe that, then we should know that God just wants what's best for us, so we should trust him and do this."

"I see someone has already been given her gifts," Padre Pio said delightedly.

"Her gifts?" Mary said. "Are we getting gifts now?"

"Yes," he replied, "if you agree to this mission, you will be well equipped. There are many gifts of the Holy Spirit, nine in particular that are very powerful and will help you immensely."

"Will we talk to angels and bilocate, like you?" Christian asked excitedly.

"I think I may be the bearer once more of those particular gifts," Padre Pio answered, "but we shall see what the Good Lord has planned. One thing is clear: your young sister here has been given both the gift of knowledge and the gift of wisdom. Those are incredible gifts for one so young to bear." Serena beamed.

"Are you all ready to join your sister and to embrace this important call?"

The children looked at one another and seemed to gain strength.

"We are," they exclaimed in unison.

"Excellent!" said Padre Pio, his eyes twinkling, "Would you like to know what gifts God has in store for each of you? They are wondrous indeed!"

"I'd like to fly!" Angelica cried out. "I'd really, really appreciate that gift!"

"I'm sorry, my dear," the saint said. "I don't believe that one's on the list, but you will be amazed at what God would like to offer you. You, Angelica, are being given the gift of miracles."

Angelica's mouth dropped open. "GET OUT!" she exclaimed. The saint looked a little confused.

Then Angelica had a thought, "Could it be the *miracle* of flying?" she asked, her eyes pleading.

The old man chuckled and answered, "We will see in what way Our Good Lord will allow this particular gift to be made manifest."

Angelica smiled. "I have no idea what that means, but it sounds cool."

One by one, Padre Pio approached the children, prayed over them, and then announced the gift that was to be given them.

To Liam was given the gift of healing; Christian received the discernment of spirits; Allora was given the gift of prophesy as well as the gift of faith.

"Mary," said Padre Pio, "to you Our Lord offers the gift of both speaking in tongues and the interpretation of tongues!"

"Wait!" Liam called out. "Tongues? Like as in languages? I think there's been a mistake, because languages are really *my* thing." His face was red with frustration and the threat of tears stung his eyes. "I just don't understand, " he said under his breath. "I should be the one being given that gift."

Mary wasn't insulted in the least. "It's true," she said. "I can't even get past the second chapter in my French primer."

"There is no mistake. Mary is an open vessel and God will be able to do great things through her." Liam remained disappointed at the saint's proclamation but accepted the verdict.

Christian placed his hand on his older brother's shoulder. "You've been given the gift of healing. That's not too shabby."

Liam perked up. "That's true," he said, "and I haven't even attended medical school yet." He gave his famous Han Solo grin.

"These gifts will be of great assistance to you, but you must further protect yourselves against the forces that will rise to meet you."

Christian thought for a moment and blurted out, "I'd like a sword and possibly a big shield, with the same impenetrable properties as Captain America's!"

The saint laughed, "You, my dear children are full of humorous and strange notions."

"Yup. We're pretty fun," Angelica declared with pride.

"You will not be given armor at this time," said Padre Pio, "but that's not to say you won't in the near future."

MYSTIC INFORMANT **31**

Christian's eyes widened. "Woo hoo!" he cried.

The saint cautioned him, "The armor you receive may not be what you are thinking. The protection I speak of at this time will come from offering acts of kindness, placing others' needs ahead of your own, and working to overcome your own faults and shortcomings. Every act, even the smallest ones of this nature, will be woven together and become a shield about you with, as you say, *impenetrable properties.*"

Christian looked disappointed. "That sounds boring."

Padre Pio looked sternly at the boy. "You will not think it boring when you are in the thick of evil, frozen in terror, and the only hope of escape will be tied to the state of your soul in that moment." Christian gulped and stepped back.

"My dear children, use this time wisely," cautioned Padre Pio. "As I have warned you, the visitor will be in your midst tomorrow and you must be ready to face her."

Christian ran toward the door. "My boy, you cannot run away from this!" the saint called out.

"I'm not!" Christian replied. "I'm going to see if the twins' diapers need to be changed. I hate changing diapers, so I figure it will be a pretty big offering and will help to protect us against the scary visitor tomorrow!"

"Well done, Christian. Well done indeed!"

CHAPTER 5

FOR THE REST OF THE DAY, THE CHILDREN worked hard to make offerings around the house.

Liam pulled out his precious Star Wars figure collection and let Joachim play with it. The three-year-old was particularly attached to the elderly Obi-Wan Kenobi character and asked innocently, "Where are his gloves?"

The girls had to work extra hard not to get into arguments. Angelica was wearing Allora's headband, but Allora used the opportunity to practice patience and not get angry. "Hey, Angelica," she said with a genuine smile, "that looks really nice on you. You can borrow it anytime you like."

Mary's offering was pretty special too. Her dog, Emma, was delivered, and as she suspected, the dryer had mangled the pretty pup's fur. Mary's eyes darted to her little sister Kiara, who was trying to stuff a sock under her Barbie doll's dress so she'd look like she was having a baby. Instead of yelling at her, she said, "Kiara, come hold Emma; she smells like strawberries and wildflowers now!"

Kiara's eyes lit up. She held Emma to her nose and sniffed. "Yum!" She looked nervously at Mary. "Mawy forgive Kia?"

"Yes!" Mary said as the little girl jumped into her arms, "I forgive you... but don't do that again."

"My won't." Kiara cheerfully replied. The toddler buried her face in Mary's sweater. "You smell yum too!"

Mary laughed. "Yeah, Angelica did my laundry for me."

The children's parents were overjoyed at the display of love and service that evening. The older children helped the younger ones get ready for bed without having to be asked and without complaint. Their mother sighed, "I feel like I'm in heaven."

Their father added, "I feel like they're up to something... but I'll take it!"

The children went to bed feeling satisfied that they had worked hard to prepare themselves, but they were still nervous about what might lie ahead. They said their prayers, and Serena added a few extra words at the end: "... and please be happy with my offering of eating the ugly mushrooms in the lasagna without making a scrunchy face. Amen."

The next morning, everyone was up earlier than usual. There was an air of suspense and uncertainty, as all of the older children were a little fearful of the impending visitor. What made it worse was that the Douglas household had more visitors that day than ever before! Every time the doorbell rang, the children froze and with wide eyes, they would timidly peek through the tall thin windows on either side of the front doors. Angelica was a little unique in her approach. She was in detective mode, which made for some interesting encounters as she questioned anyone who dared approach their home.

    The first to arrive was a teenage girl, her red hair tied in a messy low ponytail, crowned with a worn baseball cap. Angelica spoke, "You're new around here, aren't you." It

MYSTIC INFORMANT   **35**

wasn't a question, more like an accusation. The girl gave a puzzled look and handed Angelica a newspaper. She hurried away in spite of Angelica calling out after her, "Hey! We're not done here!"

The next visitor was Steve, the mailman. "Steve?" Angelica began.

"Hi, Sunshine!" he happily replied.

"You're a man, right?"

Steve looked a little confused. "Yes. Yes I am."

Angelica nodded, satisfied with his response, and said definitively, "That is all."

Steve walked away with an amused smile on his face. Angelica turned to go back inside and found her father standing in the doorway with his hands on his hips and a stern look on his face.

"What do you think you are doing?" he asked. "Please stop harassing everyone who comes to our door." Angelica gave a sheepish look, "He-he; sorry, Dad."

A pair of Jehovah's Witnesses came shortly after. They handed Mary a pamphlet and asked if she believed that God was at work in the world today. Mary's eyes shone and she said excitedly, "Yup! And don't tell anyone, but we're on a secret mission for him!" The old couple was surprised but smiled at Mary's enthusiasm. "Gotta go. VERY important matters to attend to," she said in a dramatic whisper as she closed the door.

Susan, the next-door neighbor, was their next visitor. She

was carrying a big box and said, "Here's a little treat for you children."

Normally, they were super excited when Susan brought them things, but that day, they were a little suspicious. "Thank you… " Allora said as she tentatively accepted the box. Susan headed home, and the children placed the box on the kitchen table.

"Should we open it?" Allora asked the others.

"Let me handle this," Christian said confidently, "I have a gift that might help us in this situation." He slowly opened the box and revealed its contents:

blueberry muffins.

Everyone heaved a sigh of relief. "Wait!" cried Christian, "They could be poisoned!"

Serena gasped. Christian put on his *brave face* and said, "I volunteer to sample them, for the good of our family."

Allora wasn't buying it. "You're just trying to sneak a muffin! They're probably fine. I'll even taste one to prove it."

Christian looked at his sister and with an air of condescension said, "I have been given the gift of discernment of spirits! Only I will be able to determine whether they're evil muffins or not."

"Oh brother!" Allora said, "That's not how it works." She shoved a muffin into her mouth and in a muffled voice said, "See, they're fine!" Just then, her expression changed. Her hands flew to her throat and she sank to the floor.

MYSTIC INFORMANT   **37**

CHAPTER 6

"**ALLORA!" THE CHILDREN CRIED OUT.**
Allora lay on the floor in a heap of tangled hair and muffin crumbs.

"This is terrible!" Serena squeaked, her lower lip quivering.

"Allora, while you're down there, can you scrub that patch of dried tomato sauce from last night's dinner?" their father asked as he walked past her and casually popped a smaller muffin into his mouth.

"NOOO!" the children cried out.

"What?!" he exclaimed, "Are they moldy?"

There was laughter coming from the floor. Allora stood up and said, "They're poisonous!" Their father walked away chuckling.

Angelica gave Allora a shove, yelling, "You scared me!"

Mary wanted to be mad but was too impressed with her sister's performance. "That was perfectly executed. The passion, the expressiveness, the SOUL. I've never been more proud."

Liam looked disappointed. "I was going to try out my gift of healing," he sighed. "Maybe next time."

The visitors continued to pour in. Mary suspected Miss Grassy, another neighbor who was less than neighborly. She had come by to ask them if they had seen her cat— one of about twenty but apparently a favorite.

"Her name's Duchess Thelma. She has orange freckles," she informed them. "Let me know if you see her. She's going to be grounded for running off like that!"

The children assured her they'd be on the lookout.

"It's got to be her!" Mary declared as she closed the door.

Allora didn't buy it. "She's just an old lady who likes to keep to herself."

Mary shook her head. "She holds garage sales at night. Who does that?!" she insisted. "And they're by invitation only! That's a little messed up, wouldn't you agree?"

"Okay, yes that's weird, but I'm pretty sure it's not her. She's a little crazy, but not evil."

The doorbell rang yet again.

Angelica opened the door for their next guest. It was their seventeen-year-old cousin, Kaitlyn, who had stopped by for a quick visit. Angelica eyed her suspiciously.

"Why are you looking at me like that?" Kaitlyn asked.

Angelica interrogated the teenager. "Are you secretly weaving a web that will lead to our family's ultimate ruin?"

Kaitlyn's eyes popped. "Um, no. Not that I'm aware of."

"Angelica, cut it out!" Allora called out. "Sorry, Kaitlyn; Angelica's thinks she's a detective today. She even harassed our mailman!" Their cousin laughed and promised to be on the lookout for anyone attempting to weave a web leading to the ruin of others.

They waited to see who would be their next suspect/visitor. Once more the doorbell rang out and the older girls peaked through the windows to see who had come.

"It's Morta!" Mary said excitedly. Morta was a friend of their mother's. They had been friends since college and, although the children rarely saw her, she often sent them fun and exciting gifts.

"Hey rascals! How are you guys doing?" Morta called. "Where's your mom? We are seriously overdue for a coffee date."

"Hi Morta," their mom's voice rang out as she descended their staircase. "What a wonderful surprise! I was just laying the baby down for a nap, so it's the perfect time for a coffee." She hugged her friend but was interrupted by a strange gasp.

The children turned to see Christian on the staircase. His face was pale as he stared fearfully in their direction. For a moment, he seemed to be frozen, his hand locked tightly on the rail, his knuckles white with tension. Then he shook his head a little and seemed to come to his senses. He mustered out a strange series of excuses, "I... um...sorry, I thought I saw something. I think I forgot to eat or something... I just felt a little dizzy for a moment. Maybe I'm dehydrated. I think I'm okay now, though. Sorry Morta. Hi, by the way."

Morta gave a nervous laugh and said, "It's all right Buddy." She looked at Christian with great concern. "Are you sure you're okay?"

"Yeah." He gave a feeble smile, but when Morta reached out to hug him, Christian jolted back. "Sorry; I think maybe I should go lie down," he said as he turned and bolted up the stairs.

The children's mother looked confused. "That was weird," she said. "I'll go check on him, but why don't you girls take Morta into the dining room? Allora, can you get her some coffee, please?"

"Sure Mom," Allora said, "How do you like your coffee, Morta?"

Morta didn't reply at first. Her eyes had darkened and she was staring intensely up the stairs. She caught herself and turned back to Allora, smiling sweetly. "Black, dear. Very black."

CHAPTER 7

CHRISTIAN WAS SITTING IN THE CORNER OF his bedroom, his arms locked around his knees and his head buried.

"Hey," his mother said gently as she sat down beside him. "What's going on with you?"

"I saw something and it scared me," Christian said. He looked sadly at his mom. "I thought I could be brave, but now I'm not so sure."

"Christian you are one of the bravest people I know." She thought for a moment and then asked gently, "What did you see?"

Christian looked away. "How did you meet Morta?" he asked.

"She was in my theatre program. She was always a free spirit, and we had a lot of laughs. Morta was offered an amazing opportunity right out of college. I think it was to head her own theatre company. We lost touch for many years, and I thought for sure I wouldn't see her again, but then she reached out to me a couple of years ago. She has a sister who lives near here, but I think there must have been some sort of falling out, because Morta doesn't mention her much anymore. Morta and I are very different, and we don't agree on everything, but I appreciate the effort she makes."

"Is she religious at all?"

"I've heard her say she's *spiritual*, not religious."

"I don't think I know what that means."

His mom laughed, "I'm not sure I fully understand what that means either, but I'm glad we have the opportunity to get together from time to time. I was actually surprised by her visit today; she usually likes to meet up at a coffee shop or restaurant. So I'm happy she came. I like it when she gets to spend time with my children because I think your faith makes you shine. You're all beautiful examples of God's love, and it's good for her to experience that."

"Maybe," Christian said quietly.

Christian's mom stood up and pulled her son to his feet. "Let's go. We shouldn't keep Morta waiting."

Christian was hesitant but agreed to face their visitor.

Downstairs Morta had her own line of questions.

"Wow, your brother was acting pretty strange. Any idea what would make him act that way?"

"Not sure," Mary replied, "but we've had some pretty crazy things happening lately and we're expecting some woman to…"

"MARY!" Allora interrupted, "you're supposed to check on Kiara and Joachim!"

Mary looked confused. "They're having their naps and, besides, I want to be close to the front door in case the woman…."

"NO!" Allora insisted, "I'm pretty sure Mom would appreciate it if you checked on the toddlers. Like right now. This instant. Go!"

"Fine," Mary said in a confused tone, "I'll be right back."

"Can't wait, Mary," Morta said. "You'll have to tell me more."

Morta turned her attention to Allora, Angelica, and Serena. "I have gifts for all you older girls."

"Awesome!" said Angelica, "Can we see them?"

"For sure!" Morta replied. She swept her long, dark hair behind her shoulders and pulled off her purse. She rummaged through it and then pulled out four small boxes. They were beautifully wrapped in shiny black paper and topped with silky red bows.

"So pretty!" said Angelica, "Which one's mine?"

"You can pick one," Morta said. "They're all the same. I just know you're going to love them!"

The girls each took a box and opened it. Allora was more

hesitant in opening her gift, as she was still spooked by Christian's expression on the staircase. She kept thinking about Padre Pio's description of the woman who would be visiting. He had said she would be all goodness but wasn't to be trusted. He had said that she wasn't what she seemed. Was there any way that the woman could be someone they already knew, someone who had already secured their trust? Was it possible that Morta was the woman with a dark plan to hurt their family?

"EEEEEK!" Angelica squealed with excitement, "It's so beautiful!" She held up the gift from Morta: a beautiful necklace with a large crystal charm. "Thank you, Morta!"

Morta smiled warmly, "You should try it on."

"Stop!" Allora cried. Morta shot her a questioning look. "We should wait for Mom. Besides, Mary hasn't gotten to open hers yet and it will ruin the surprise."

Angelica frowned, but begrudgingly obeyed her sister.

Christian and his mother soon made their way into the dining room, apologizing for the delay. Christian wouldn't look at Morta, but her green eyes were locked on him.

"Are you feeling any better?" she asked, her voice soft with concern.

Christian nodded his head, still refusing to meet her gaze.

"I hope Mary comes back soon, so you girls can all try on your gifts," Morta said excitedly.

"Morta, you shouldn't have," their mother said. "You're always so generous."

"What gifts?" Christian asked, growing pale again.

Angelica lifted up her necklace. The crystal caught the light from a window and cast a strange greenish glow against the wall. Christian took a step back and his eyes widened with fear.

"That's pretty," said their mother.

"I should've gotten one for you, too, so you could match the girls."

"That's all right, you know I prefer my crucifix."

Morta wrinkled her nose. "One day we'll have to get you to upgrade to something a little fancier."

"Oh, I don't know about that," their mother insisted. Then she turned to Allora. "Sweetie, can you go find Mary? I'm sure your sisters are eager to try on their necklaces."

Allora nodded and dashed up the stairs. She had an eerie feeling about the necklaces and wanted to make sure she had a chance to brief Mary about her concerns. Mary was just starting down the stairs.

"Mary!," Allora urgently whispered. "Something's not right! I think Morta may be the woman Padre Pio was speaking about."

"Impossible," Mary answered. "We've known her for years. She's Mom's friend, not to mention the fact that she always gives us gifts."

"But what if we were only fooled into thinking she was a friend. Didn't you see Christian's face? I think his *spidey sense* has been taken to a whole new level. Remember, he's been given the gift of discernment of spirits and he can't even look at her. And there's something strange about the gifts she's brought us."

Mary's face lit up, "She brought us more gifts??"

"Mary, snap out of it! I don't think they're "nice" gifts; I have a feeling they might be... evil or something. They've got Christian really freaked out."

Mary's eyes grew serious. "This is not good. I wish Padre Pio was here. Didn't he say he'd be with us?"

"Yes, but he said he wouldn't be here for the entirety of the task.

"I'm scared, Allora."

"I know. Me too. But we have to make sure the other girls don't try on the necklaces, and we need to figure out a way to get Morta out of our house."

"We need to come up with a plan."

Mary's eyes widened as she looked over Allora's shoulder and saw the figure standing near the bottom of the stairs. A pair of green eyes narrowed in on the girls, their gaze cold and piercing. As Allora turned and faced Morta, her breath caught in her throat.

CHAPTER 8

HOW MUCH HAD MORTA HEARD? IT SEEMED AS though she must have heard enough to know the girls were onto her.

The doorbell rang yet again. This time, its tones were sweet and heavenly to the girls' ears. Morta hurried back into the dining room while Allora and Mary ran toward the door singing, "We'll get it!"

They threw the door open and almost leapt for joy at the sight of Padre Pio. He wasn't dressed in his brown robe, though; he was dressed in a plaid shirt and pleated pants. He looked... ordinary somehow. He carried a small, flat slab of wood. It bore an image of Mary, the Mother of God, framed with painted gold edges. He flashed a smile and then winked as if to encourage the girls to keep his true identity a secret. Their mother joined them at the door.

"Hello," she greeted him. "You must be from the church."

Padre Pio nodded and smiled warmly, "You signed up to be part of the shrine apostolate. I hope you don't mind, but I took the liberty of delivering it to you so you could begin your time with this holy image a little early. I know you have a lot on the go with your big, beautiful family."

"How thoughtful," she replied, "It has been a really busy day, so I appreciate that!"

"What's a *Shrine Aposto... aposta*?" Mary asked.

"Apostolate," her mother corrected her. "This beautiful picture of Mother Mary travels from home to home, and the families who receive the image pray together and receive many graces and blessings through Mary's intercession." She turned to the old man. "Thank you so much for bringing it to us."

"Would you like to come in for some tea or coffee?" Allora blurted out. Her mother seemed surprised at her daughter's invitation but was proud of her warmth and hospitality.

"Yes, please come in," she said. "We'll prepare a place of honor for the shrine."

Allora was overjoyed as the saint nodded and carried the beautiful image into their home.

They rounded the corner and entered the dining room.

The encounter was almost electric in nature. The moment Morta looked up into the eyes of the saint, she jumped. Her eyes filled with panic and her breath became short and stagnant.

"How... what are you... I... " Morta's eyes darted toward her friend, who looked both concerned and confused. Morta seemed to catch herself and attempted to regain her composure.

"Hello there," she said to the man, without looking him in the eye. He took a step toward her and she winced, stepping back. She noted the image in his hands and took another step back, looking nauseated and fearful.

"I'm happy to meet you," Padre Pio said in an authoritative tone. "I've brought this holy image for this family to keep in their home. Isn't it lovely? It will remain here for a good duration." His words seemed a warning to the woman, who nodded and attempted to smile, but her face was partly twisted with a look of disgust. Morta clumsily began to gather up her belongings. "I don't mean to be rude, but I should probably get going," she spat out.

Padre Pio stared at her with great intensity. "Can I help you carry anything? Perhaps these lovely necklaces?" Rage flashed for a moment in her eyes.

"Oh, my friend brought those as gifts for our girls," the children's mother explained.

The old man stared deep into Morta's eyes, almost asserting a command. She shrunk under his unmoving gaze.

"Actually," she said feebly, "I noticed that there are some flaws in the crystals. If you don't mind, I'd like to take them back and have them repaired. I hope you girls aren't too disappointed."

"Oh, believe me, we're not!" Mary triumphantly declared.

Morta's eyes narrowed at Mary's words, and she clumsily gathered up the necklaces, her face contorted and pasty white. She hurried toward the door, calling back, "Sorry again to rush off, I'll call you sometime this week."

"Well that was strange," the children's mother remarked. "I've never known Morta to act like that. I hope she's not sick. Poor thing!"

Christian looked at his mother and said in earnest, "She's definitely sick."

Just then a loud voice called out with squeal of joy.

"OBI WAN!!!"

Joachim had woken from his nap and was running into the room. His arms flailing excitedly, he threw himself into the arms of the saint, hugging him with all his strength. The boy lifted his head and, looking into his dear friend's face, innocently inquired, "Why are you dressed funny?"

"Oh, Sweetie!" his mother laughed apologetically. "He's not Obi-Wan; he's a nice man from our church." The other children laughed. He was indeed a nice man from their Church!

"Although," she said, "you actually remind me of one of my favorite saints: Padre Pio. You must get that a lot."

The old man laughed and nodded. She continued, "He's always been like a spiritual father to me."

The saint's eyes sparkled, "I'm sure he considers you a spiritual daughter."

"That makes us kind of like, *spiritual grandchildren!*"

Serena cried out.

"Yes, it does," the old man concurred.

Just then, Liam walked in, his face buried in a medical encyclopedia. He looked up from his book and stopped dead in his tracks when he saw the saint in civilian clothing, standing in his dining room and surrounded by his family, their faces still flushed with excitement.

"What'd I miss?!" he asked, his face a perfect picture of confusion.

"You have no idea…" Serena mumbled under her breath.

The disguised saint joined the children for some refreshments. Allora brought him a small cup of espresso and whispered, "You're Italian, right? I heard Italians really like this stuff."

Padre Pio nodded, "Oh yes!"

"I hear the twins stirring," their mom said. "Allora, can you help me get them out of their cribs?"

Allora nodded and they headed upstairs accompanied by Joachim, who said, "I'll be right back so don't go away!"

Allora added, "And please don't say anything too interesting while we're gone!" Their mother laughed and motioned them to continue.

In spite of Allora's request, the other children couldn't help themselves and used the opportunity to talk about their secret mission with the saint.

"That was crazy!" Angelica said, her eyes wide. "I can't believe Morta is so bad!"

Padre Pio shook his head, "She wasn't always, but she has ventured down a very dark path and she has been... consumed. I think Christian understands why."

"What did you see, Christian?" Mary asked.

"I saw two dark figures, one on either side of her. Their hands were more like claws, and they were buried in Morta's shoulders. The crazy thing is that she didn't seem to mind; it was like they were a part of her—an extension of her body. And the crystals from the necklaces... the dark figures were drawn to them, like magnets. I don't know what would have happened if the girls had put them on, but I knew it wouldn't be good."

Serena hid her face in her hands. Padre Pio put his arm around her. "You prepared your hearts well with your frequent acts of selflessness. It is how the Holy Spirit was able to ensure your protection against this evil. You need not fear if you remain close to his heart. Also, I have gifts for you that will be a wonderful help in further protecting you."

Serena held out her hand and the saint shook his head. "Your gifts will come as they so often do, through the inspiration of the Holy Spirit, from those holy souls who are open to doing his will."

"I'm not sure I know what that means," Serena said.

"You will," he replied.

Christian was comforted by the saint's words but was still disturbed by all that he had seen. He had a thought. "You should follow Morta to see where's she's going and what she's up to!"

Padre Pio nodded. "I agree. That's why I am, right at this very moment in fact!"

Angelica's eyes widened. "You're bilocating??" she asked, flabbergasted. "Awesome!"

"I'm not alone," the saint added. "I'm getting Liam up to speed."

Liam had been sitting beside Padre Pio. He hadn't peeped a word, and he showed both surprise and wonder. He muttered, "I'm... I'm with him... both here... and there!"

"WHERE??!" Mary cried out, unable to stand the suspense.

CHAPTER 9

MORTA HURRIED THROUGH THE SMALL TOWN just south of the Douglas home.

She was in a state of fury and confusion. Her visit had not gone as planned, and she was not looking forward to having to face the one many referred to as *The Devourer*. Morta was so focused on her upcoming encounter that she didn't notice that she was being followed.

Padre Pio and his young companion remained at a distance and watched as Morta ventured through an alleyway and then stopped at a large, wooden door between two dumpsters. She glanced around cautiously before producing a key and unlocking the door. She slipped through the doorway, and the door slowly began to close behind her. The saint managed to catch the door before it snapped shut. After waiting a few minutes, he and Liam made their way into the building. Turning to Liam, Padre Pio whispered urgently, "We must try to be as quiet as possible."

There was a tunnel that seemed like the inside of a dragon's throat. Echoes of water dripping and faint cries could be heard in the distance. It was unusually hot and lit only by a series of small red sconces that lined the wall and led the visitors deep into the tunnel. It sloped steeply downward, and the rocky ground glistened from the moisture.

"Careful," the saint whispered, cautioning his companion, "the surface is somewhat slippery." Liam nodded and kept one hand on the wall beside him. The other grasped the saint's habit as he led the way. They soon sensed they were approaching the end of the tunnel, as the air became thick

MYSTIC INFORMANT   **57**

with an odorous heat. It made Liam feel uneasy, sickened with fear. They could hear a deep voice bellowing from within, throbbing with rage, as Morta's thin voice pleaded.

"They knew! I don't know how, but they knew. It's not my fault!" she cried.

"How many years have we been preparing for this?" the voice sneered. "You were to ensure that they would wear the crystals. It was a simple task!"

"But the boy!" she insisted. "He knew! He could see everything beyond the temporary reality. You should have warned me this could have happened!"

"DON'T YOU DARE REPRIMAND ME, MAGGOT!!!" Morta let out a whimper.

Padre Pio and Liam remained hidden in the tunnel as the argument continued.

"I did everything I could, and I almost managed to secure the girls, in spite of the boy. The plan would still have worked, if it weren't for... him!"

"WHO?!" the voice roared.

Morta took a deep breath. "The children are being protected by a saint."

"You've encountered saints before and still managed to pull souls from their grip."

"This is not an earthly saint, still on his own journey. This is a heavenly saint, obviously appointed as a guardian. And this particular saint even thwarted you during his earthly life."

"The white robed man? The grey?"

"Brown robe."

"NOOOO! Not him!!!"

"And what's worse is he's brought a powerful holy item into their home, so I won't be able to get in there until it's removed."

"Well then, find a way to lure them out! Or you can bet you'll never... "

The dark voice stopped short as though something had alerted him to the presence of the outsiders. He growled, "YOU FOOL! You've been followed!!!"

CHAPTER 10

PADRE PIO'S EYES POPPED OPEN, AS DID Liam's, and the children surrounding them leaned in with concern.

"What is it? What happened?" they asked all at once.

"We had to abandon the mission," he sighed. "It seems an old enemy of mine was able to sense our presence. But not to worry, we are now able to reveal more information to you about the plan they have for your family."

"They?" asked Angelica. "One scary woman was bad enough."

"I speak of Morta and the one she answers to," Padre Pio replied.

"Who's that?" Serena asked fearfully.

"We will speak more of this later," the saint answered. "As for now, I implore you to make more small, but powerful, offerings within the home. Even the smallest sacrifice made with great love will provide extraordinary graces. They will serve as a strong defense against this evil."

He smiled quite suddenly, as though alerted to someone's presence. "Oh! It seems the gifts I have been preparing for you have arrived."

Just then there was a knock at the door. The children all ran to the front foyer and excitedly flung the door open. Their visitor jumped a little at the force.

"Oh, hello!" she said with a big smile. It was Mrs. Berry, one of the kind ladies from their church. "I was running some errands and wanted to drop off a little gift for you all. I've had them for awhile now, but this morning, I especially had it on my heart to get them to you."

She held out her hand, and the children were delighted to see the gifts in her hand: small, shiny silver crosses. "They're pretty special," she continued. "They are scapular medals; they have beautiful medals embedded in them: the Miraculous Medal, the image of the Sacred Heart of Jesus, and the medals of Our Lady of Mount Carmel, St. Joseph, and St. Benedict as well as the guardian angels in the center of the cross. Oh, and they've been blessed too! I hope you like them."

"You have no idea!" Angelica exclaimed.

The children were giddy with excitement and gratitude and hugged the dear woman, thanking her for being so good to them. She bid them goodbye, and the children ran back toward the dining room to show Padre Pio (and to thank him too).

But he was gone.

"Who was at the door?" they heard their mother enquire as she descended the stairs, holding one of the twins.

"And where's Padre... " Allora caught herself, "... that nice man from church?"

"Where's MY OBI-WAN??" Joachim added despairingly.

"I guess he had to go," Christian said with a sigh, "but the visitor at the door was Mrs. Berry, and look at what she brought us!!!"

"Oh how thoughtful," said their mother, approaching the crosses. The baby in her arms, James, tried to grab them. Jacinta, who was at her side, tugged on her pant leg.

"No," their mother told them, "you'll just try to eat them. They're for your older brothers and sisters." James let out a wail.

"He cries like Chewbacca!" Joachim said with a frown.

"Let's go find some toys for the twins in the playroom." She led Joachim and the twins out of the foyer.

Allora turned to her siblings, "Soooo... anything *interesting* happen while I was upstairs?"

Angelica answered excitedly, "You could say that! Liam will probably be able to tell us more about it."

Allora looked a little hurt. She hated to miss out on anything *exciting*, so she put on her authoritative face and said firmly, "LCAMAS meeting pronto!"

"But the clubhouse is still... missing a floor," Serena

reminded her.

"Oh yeah," said Allora. "We'll have to come up with a new meeting place."

Liam thought for a moment. He was reminded of the words spoken by the dark voice and the plan to try and lure them out of the home.

"We should choose a place we can meet that's inside the house," he said.

"Why?" asked Mary.

"Just trust me," Liam answered, "and I have the perfect spot in mind." He gave Christian a look that seemed to say *it's time*.

"NO!" Christian said in a panic, "We agreed to keep it secret! If we show them now, we won't have any place to go when we're trying to escape the girls!!"

"I know it's a sacrifice, but I think it's important. Besides, didn't Padre Pio say that the more sacrifices we can make for others, the better? It will make us stronger if we ever have to face..."

"WHO? WHAT??" Mary cried out.

"Never mind," said Liam. "Come on! Christian, lead the way."

Christian led the group upstairs and down the hallway to the last room on the right: his bedroom. The two oldest boys shared a room with Joachim, and shortly after they had moved in, they had found a small, secret hatch in the floor of their closet. They discovered it when they had tried to convince Joachim that their closet was really a swimming pool. He had believed them and tried to fill up the swimming pool with real water using a small cup. As punishment, their father had entrusted them with the unfavorable task of cleaning up the mess. As they peeled the wet carpet back, they had come across the small wooden door in the floor with a metal handle.

Christian turned to the girls, "You can come in, but you can't tell anyone else about this and you can't just come in here whenever you want!" The girls nodded their heads and solemnly promised to respect the boys' wishes.

Christian pulled the hatch open and climbed down a short ladder. It led to a small opening: a type of crawl space between their floor and the ceiling below. There was just enough room for all the children to sit comfortably without bumping their heads.

"The dining room's just below us; that's why the ceiling in the dining room is a little lower than the ceilings in the rest of the house."

"This is awesome!" Angelica cried out, a large smile plastered across her face.

"We should get started," Allora said. "Liam, you can call us to order this time, if you want."

Liam adjusted his glasses and called out, "Order! At this meeting we'll be discussing the impending danger that lurks beyond the borders of this house, the plot to wrap peculiar, malevolent crystals (with powers yet to be fully revealed) around our necks, and the extreme measures of defense that will need to be taken as we face this mysterious, ominous force of darkness!"

Mary's jaw dropped, "And they say that *I'm* the dramatic one!"

"Liam," Serena said in her *teacher's tone*, "small words please."

"Okay," Liam said, "on my journey bilocating with Padre Pio..."

"That is so cool!" Angelica couldn't help interrupting, "Sorry, please continue."

"We followed Morta to a secret place where she was meeting a... well, we couldn't see him, but I think he was some kind of dark boss. He told her that she had failed, because her mission was to get the girls to wear the crystals. She told him about Padre Pio; she knew exactly who he was! And she also said that she can't come into our house as long as the shrine is being kept here."

"I wish we could keep it forever!" Mary said.

"I think the next family is scheduled to pick it up tomorrow afternoon," Allora said disappointedly.

"Well, it doesn't really matter because I don't think they're going to wait until it's gone," Liam cautioned, "Morta's boss instructed her to try and lure us outside of the home."

"Not going to happen!" Christian said firmly.

"But it is," sighed Allora, "We have swimming lessons tomorrow... unless we can come up with an excuse, like saying we're feeling sick."

"I don't think anyone would believe that all six of us just happened to get sick at the same time," insisted Liam. "Besides, I have a feeling that lying would only make the force we're up against stronger, so we'll just have to find a way to protect ourselves."

"I don't like this," Serena said frowning.

CHAPTER 11

THE NEXT DAY, THE CHILDREN TRIED TO perform more acts of kindness. Serena helped Joachim get dressed and offered to make everyone's bed. Allora had a special offering that she was sure would have a huge impact. She opened up her jewelry box. It was filled with beautiful beaded necklaces that she had made over the years as well as various chains and jewels that she had received as gifts. She hated dismantling the precious items, but she knew it would make the offering all the sweeter. She worked swiftly, her fingers meticulously crafting new articles, a swirl of colorful gems and flashes of silver. Soon, Allora stood up with a contented smile on her face. Her works of love were ready for delivery.

"Here's your swimsuit, Mary," she said happily as she tossed the rolled-up garment to her sister.

Mary had a look of dread on her face. "How can you be so happy, when this swimsuit represents our departure from the safety of our home?"

"Open it up," Allora insisted.

Mary unrolled her swimsuit and found one of Allora's beautifully altered necklaces. It had dark blue and teal beads, and at the center was one of the silver crosses that Mrs. Berry had given them.

Mary smiled and said, "Yes! Thank you, Allora! I feel much better now!"

Allora delivered a necklace to each of her siblings. She had even made one for Joachim that was almost indestructible (she knew it would have to be if he were to wear it for more than a day). She had chosen thick chains for the boys, and they were grateful she hadn't tried to make them wear the ones with flowery or heart-shaped beads.

Their mother called the children to come to the foyer. She wasn't wearing her shoes or carrying her purse.

"Aren't you taking us to swimming lessons?" Liam asked.

"I'm so sorry, guys," she said, "but I have an unexpected appointment. But don't worry, someone else has offered to drive you. You won't believe it, but Morta called this morning. She's feeling much better today and said she would love to spend some more time with you!"

Allora's heart sank. All that effort to protect her siblings and they were being sent straight into the arms of the very one who would cause them harm. Their mother saw the fear in the eyes of the children looking back at her.

"What's going on?" she asked.

"We can't go with Morta. We can't explain right now, but we have to be honest with you and..." Allora's eyes filled with tears, "we just can't go with her."

Their mother was deeply concerned. "Okay," she said, "I can cancel my appointment... or, if you'd like, I could ask Kaitlyn to take you. Your dad will stay here with the five youngest. Would that be all right?"

The children looked at each other and nodded.

"I'll give Kaitlyn a call, but we'll need to talk about this later. Agreed?"

"Agreed," they said.

Their mother left to make the call. "That was close," Liam said, "Morta's getting bolder."

"We'll have to take extra care anytime we leave the house!" Allora said.

The doorbell rang and Mary peaked out the side window.

"It's Morta!" she announced. "What should we do?"

Christian was surprisingly calm. "Open the door," he said, "and try to stay calm, but don't step out of the house."

Mary tentatively opened the door. "Hi Morta," she said with a forced smile. "How are you?"

"Good!" Morta said warmly, "I'm so excited to spend some time with you guys today!"

Christian stared steadily at the visitor. "You should come in," he said, raising an eyebrow. He was curious to see how

MYSTIC INFORMANT   **69**

she would respond. She returned his stare and stated calmly, "I'm good here. Plus, I think we should get going. I wouldn't want you to be late for your lessons. Your mom said we can take your van."

"Actually," Liam said, "I think our cousin, Kaitlyn is going to drive us."

"It's true," they heard their mother say as she entered the foyer. "I'm so sorry, Morta. I would have contacted you sooner, but as it turns out, their cousin is going to take them. I'm so sorry for the inconvenience. We'll just have to plan to get together some other time."

Morta closed her eyes for a moment. Her face was strained with frustration. But then, all at once her eyes opened and it looked as though she was trying hard not to smile.

"I understand," she said, "although... you may want to call her cell, sometimes young drivers can have... incidents that prevent them from following through."

Their mother looked perturbed. "What a strange thing to say," she commented. "Kaitlyn's very responsible, and she lives fairly close by... but I guess I could give her a call again and make sure everything's okay." She left the children once more to make the call.

Morta waited for her friend to leave the room and then continued. "Car rides, even short distances, can be very dangerous. Especially if someone were to experience malfunctions with her brakes... or worse still, if she were to encounter another vehicle with a dangerous driver," her lips curved into a half-smile as she finished her thought, "... a VERY dangerous driver who could run her straight off the road."

Serena gasped and grabbed onto Christian's leg.

"She'll be fine," Allora said fervently. "She will be protected and will arrive here safely... maybe just a few minutes late." Her special gift was being realized, and Allora drew great comfort knowing that all would be well somehow.

Mary on the other hand, was in a daze, her mouth frozen with a look of astonishment. She could feel someone calling out to her. Perhaps Liam would not be the only one to go on a special, bilocating journey with their saintly friend.

CHAPTER 12

ALL AT ONCE MARY WAS STANDING NEXT TO Padre Pio at the side of a road. She recognized it: McConkey Road— the very road she knew Kaitlyn would have to take to get to their home. Padre Pio turned to her and said, "We have some business to attend to. Quickly, run down the road and you will find a wooden gate. It's locked, but is quite worn. You must open it. Your guardian angel is here with you, and he will help you in your effort. Once the gate has been opened, I want you to duck behind the large boulder that will be on your right, close to the oak tree. She mustn't see you. I'll take care of the rest."

Mary was stunned. "I don't understand."

"Go now!" the saint insisted, "They'll be here within the next minute."

Mary ran as fast as she could down the road until she

spotted the old wooden gate. She pressed against it with all her might, but it wouldn't budge. "If you're here," she called out, "I'd appreciate a little help!"

She shoved the gate once more, feeling the presence of an extra set of hands beside hers. She could see a flash of light, as the gates blasted open. "Thank you, angel!" Mary said delightedly.

In the far distance, she saw Kaitlyn's car coming down the road. It hadn't reached Padre Pio yet, but Mary could see that Kaitlyn was being followed by another car. It was black with darkened windows. The car's tires squealed, as the driver seemed to be speeding up. It pulled up beside Kaitlyn's car and was about to slam into her. Kaitlyn swerved to avoid the collision and the car sped ahead of her, leaving her spinning uncontrollably in a cloud of dust. She tried to recover, but seemed to be having trouble slowing down and breaking out of the spin. Mary couldn't believe her eyes as she saw the same flash of light that had helped her open the gate now behind Kaitlyn's car, steadying and straightening the raging vehicle. Then she saw Padre Pio motioning to Kaitlyn to drive toward the gate. Mary found the boulder by the tree and quickly ducked behind it.

Kaitlyn veered her car through the gate onto the worn path beyond. The path led up a small hill which helped slow the car to a stop. Padre Pio hurried to Kaitlyn and asked the stunned driver if she was all right. She was visibly shaken.

"That was crazy! I thought I was going to crash!" she said, as she turned to the old man. "Thank you for pointing this path out to me. I never noticed it before and I don't know how I else I would've stopped. I don't know why my brakes weren't working." The old man smiled sympathetically. "I'm so sorry you had to go through that terrible ordeal. You must have been so scared. If you'll permit me, I'll have a look at your brakes," he said. "I'm sure I'll have you safely on your way in no time."

"Thank you," Kaitlyn sighed.

Mary peeked out from behind the rock and was astonished to see the saint hunched under the hood of the car. Within minutes, she saw him closing the hood and assuring Kaitlyn that she was safe to continue on her way.

Morta frowned; she didn't like the look in Mary's eyes.

"Wow!" Mary said with a smile, "that was amazing!"

Everyone turned to Mary, baffled by the girl's comment.

Mary shook her head a little and said, "Allora was right! She was protected! Kaitlyn's almost here."

Anger flashed in Morta's eyes and she blurted out, "What do you mean? How could you know... " Her voice trailed off as a car pulled into the driveway.

Kaitlyn's blue eyes sparkled as she jumped out of the car, "Hey guys! Sorry I'm a little late. Are you ready for your lessons?"

Morta seemed surprised to see the teenager. "Kaitlyn! Wow, you've really grown since I last saw you! I hope your drive over here was... uneventful."

"Actually, it wasn't," Kaitlyn said. "Some crazy driver tried to run me off the road and my brakes weren't working."

"Oh?" Morta said dryly. "It's a wonder you made it here safely."

"I know! But, almost out of nowhere there was this old man who helped me. He must have been a mechanic, too, because it took him like a couple of minutes to check my brakes and get me back out onto the road."

"Amazing!" Angelica said. Then she had a thought. "Did he happen to look a little like Padre Pio?"

Kaitlyn laughed, "Actually, yeah; he kind of did!"

"I thought so," Angelica said with a proud smile.

"We should get going!" Kaitlyn advised, "I don't want you guys to be late for your lessons."

Their mother returned and handed the van keys to Kaitlyn saying, "Thank you, Kaitlyn." She then turned to Morta and said, "You should come inside for a cup of coffee. I still have about fifteen minutes before I have to head off for my appointment."

Morta declined and kept her eyes on Kaitlyn, clearly annoyed at her presence. The children were a little nervous about stepping out of their home but were reassured by Christian.

"Let's go everyone," he said. "Morta, have we shown you our new necklaces?" He pulled out the chain from under his shirt. The silver cross caught a ray of light from the sun and seem to hit Morta square in the eyes. She squinted and took a step back.

"Lovely," she said. "I should go." The other children caught on to the woman's aversion to their new accessories.

"Look at mine!" Serena cried cheerfully.

"Yes," said Angelica, "and mine, but make sure you take a close look at all details. We've been told that these crosses have very beautiful and powerful medals embedded in them."

All the children approached Morta fearlessly, and she cowered back with her hands up saying, "I really have to go..." But the children surrounded her, and Morta could no longer feign simple disinterest. "GET AWAY FROM ME, YOU LITTLE BRATS!!!" she screamed. Her face had taken on an almost demonic appearance.

"MORTA!" their mother cried out. "What is going on here?!"

Morta sneered, "You will not continue to be thorns in the side of the true master. You will not succeed in your attempt to keep his power at bay. He will squash you, effortlessly snuffing out your light."

Serena stepped forward and firmly declared, "Your master is NOT the true Master."

"And we know how this all ends," Allora added. "We know who has the victory."

The two girls were emboldened, assured through the spiritual gifts they had been given. Their confidence baited Morta, who cringed and was compelled to reveal her true nature.

"We will see," she snarled, her expression that of a twisted, trapped animal. *"Beidh tú a scriosadh roimh Leagann ghrian."* In almost a flash, she was in her car, wheels squealing, as she sped away from the Douglas home.

"What did she say? What did those weird words mean?" Angelica asked, turning to Liam.

Liam shook his head, "I have no idea. That sounds like an old Pagan language."

"She said, *You will be destroyed before the sun sets!*" Mary said. Everyone looked at her in shock. Mary shrugged her shoulders, "I don't know how I know, but that's what she said."

"Mary," Allora said, "it's your gift from the Holy Spirit! That's awesome... although, what she said... not so awesome."

"WHOA!" Kaitlyn said. "This is pretty much the craziest day I've ever had."

"We've had crazier," Angelica said matter-of-factly.

"That was scary," their mother said shaking her head. "I can't believe... I just... this is so disturbing."

She turned her attention to her children, "I'm cancelling my appointment and I think it best you stay home from your lessons. Kaitlyn, do you think you and your mother would be okay to watch our youngest five for a little while? I think the older children and their father and I will need some uninterrupted time to talk about what's been going on."

"Sure," said Kaitlyn, "I'd love to help out. Is it okay if I take them to the park first?" Kaitlyn asked her aunt. "I think my brothers are already there, and it would be a fun distraction for the littles."

"That sounds like a great idea," her aunt replied.

CHAPTER 13

K**AITLYN AND THE OLDER CHILDREN LOADED** the littles into the van, and Kaitlyn assured them that she would take good care of them.

"Noooo," Joachim asserted, "I will take care of YOU!"

Kaitlyn laughed and said, "Of course you will."

Kiara also had to add her two cents, "I take care of Emma." The doggie still looked extra puffy from its time in the dryer. Allora handed Kaitlyn a diaper bag filled with sippy cups and bottles for the littles and leaned over the car seat of the smallest member of the Douglas family, softly kissing her on the head.

"You'll be safe, don't worry," she whispered to the drowsy baby, who yawned softly. "We'll see you very soon." The children waved goodbye to their little siblings as the van rolled away.

Once back inside their home, the rest of the Douglas family congregated in the living room for their talk.

"I think we should pray our Rosary early today," their mother said. She was still a little shaken after seeing the dark side of someone she had grown to love and trust.

The prayer seemed to bring peace to the family, and as they finished, a little voice spoke up.

"It all started with that *mysterious* key." Serena was wide-eyed, lifting up her hands and wiggling her fingers, as if she were conducting a magical symphony.

Their mother couldn't help but laugh. "What key?"

"This key," Allora said, stepping forward and producing the object from her pocket.

Their parents leaned forward, examining the beautiful piece. All at once they both gasped.

"It couldn't be," their father exclaimed. "How is this possible? It's our wedding key."

"WHAT?" The children all called out at once.

Their mother took the key from Allora for a closer inspection. "Yes, this is it! Patrick, can you believe this?!"

"I don't understand," Allora said, "I found this key near the grotto, and it opened a miraculous door which started us on this crazy adventure... "

"I'm not surprised," her father interrupted. "We first saw this key on our wedding day. There was a mysterious woman who had attended. She gave us something very special that day."

They remembered it vividly. Cream-colored roses

adorned the altar, colorful beams of light shone through the rich stained glass windows, and the young couple were both aglow, having just been joined together in the Sacrament of Matrimony. Most of their guests had headed off to the reception hall while the wedding party stayed behind for pictures. The newlyweds took a moment to pray before the tabernacle, as their photographer shot photos of their little flower girl, who was affectionately hugging a statue of Mary.

The couple felt a soft touch on their shoulders. The source was a gentle hand extending from a young woman with dark hair and kind, warm eyes. She was wearing a long pale blue dress and a soft, yellow shawl.

"Excuse me," she whispered, "I'm so sorry to interrupt your time before Our Lord, but I wanted to make sure you received this gift. It's very special. In truth, it is a treasure!" She held out a chest about the size of a shoebox. It appeared ancient. It was a heavy, metallic structure with ornate patterns and strange writing.

"Thank you," Patrick said as he took the mysterious box. He tried to open it but found it was locked.

The woman smiled, "I'm sorry, but unfortunately, you will not be able to open it for many years. The box will serve an important purpose, but you will not understand its nature until its key finds you."

She held out the strange key, slowly rotating it in a stream of light. "This key will come to you exactly when you need it. It will be a time when your family is being tested."

MYSTIC INFORMANT

Her smile grew wider, "Your family will have significantly increased in size by that time!"

She wrapped her shawl around the key, and it seemed to disappear. She blessed them and bid them goodbye. The young couple were bewildered by the exchange, but ensured that the box was put in a safe place, preparing for the day it would be reunited with the mysterious key.

The children's mother became giddy with excitement. "I can't believe the day has finally come!" She ran out of the room and returned within minutes, carrying her treasure chest. "The suspense has been killing me over the years! It's time; it's finally time!"

The children laughed at the sight of their mother who was almost bobbing up and down with anticipation, her hand shaking as she grasped the key. Their mother turned to her husband with a bright smile. "Are you ready for this?"

He laughed, "Let's do it!"

She sat down beside her husband on the grey over-stuffed sofa and hesitated for a moment. "I'm actually a little nervous. Maybe we should turn the key together."

"You're killing us! Just open it!!!" Angelica cried out. She then remembered who she was addressing and added, "Please and thank you."

Her father gave her a stern look, but only momentarily, as he was just as excited as their mother. Together, the couple placed their hands on the key, turning it slowly. There was a spark of light as the chest sprung open.

"AHHH!" Their mother jumped and almost dropped the chest. "WHOA! What was that?!"

"It's normal," Mary replied matter-of-factly. "Actually, it's a bit disappointing. I was really hoping for a huge shot of lightning, like when we first used the key," she sighed dramatically, "but I guess it just wasn't meant to be."

The couple peered inside the chest. It was lined with scarlet-colored silk. A gold, antique crucifix lay at the bottom.

"How beautiful!" their mother said, and then, "Wait, what's this?"

She lifted the cross from the box and found two envelopes underneath. One was inscribed, *For Mr. & Mrs. Douglas, Humble Servants of Our Lord*. The other shocked the family. It simply read: *Morta*.

"Um, that's pretty weird," Christian commented.

"Open your envelope, right now!!!" Angelica ordered.

Her father gave her another look of disapproval.

"Please and thank you," Angelica added meekly.

Her father turned his attention back to the envelope, and carefully breaking the wax seal that had been pressed across the opening, he pulled out a folded piece of parchment.

The couple silently read the contents of their letter and then sat quietly staring at one another.

"What? WHAT?!" Mary inquired with great intensity. She couldn't stand the magnitude of mystery.

"Whoa, that's intense," their mother said, "but at least we now know how to proceed."

"HOW?!" Mary exclaimed.

Her mother gave a sympathetic look, "I'm sorry, but we've been given our own instructions. You will continue to be guided, and you don't need to worry about anything. Trust that God has his hand over you and he'll make sure you know exactly what to do. As for your father and I, we have our own mission. Just know that you won't be alone."

"So you're not going to show us what's written on your parchment?" Allora said, her face filled with disappointment.

"No," her father said gently, "except for the last few lines. But don't be afraid."

The couple looked at each other and nodded. They folded the parchment back revealing only the four bottom lines:

YOUR OFFSPRING WILL FIND REFUGE IN PIO'S CAVERN. THERE WILL THEY FLY WHEN EVIL CASTS ITS GLOW UPON THE CROSS, AND THERE THEY WILL SUMMON THE STRENGTH NEEDED TO DEFEAT THE ENEMY.

Just then, the doorbell rang and everyone jumped a little.

"I wonder who that could be," Liam said nervously.

Christian ran to the door and called out, "It's the Brydsons. I think they're here to... oh, no. They're here to pick up the shrine."

Angelica ran to the dining room and grabbed the image of Our Lady. She locked her arms around it and said firmly, "Just let them try to take it from me!"

"Angelica," her mother said in a sympathetic tone, "you need to hand it over. Don't worry, everything will be all right."

Angelica begrudgingly brought the image to the door and handed it to one of her dear friends, Anna. Anna was seven years old, and with her light blonde hair and smiley eyes, she looked like a ball of sunshine. Angelica just couldn't be upset with her.

"Here you go," she said, "Enjoy basking in its protection." Anna looked confused.

"Um, okay!" she said with a bright smile.

The little girl waved as she ran down the driveway to her family's van. The Douglas children waved back, but then they stopped short when they spotted Morta's car parked on the side of the road, just opposite their driveway.

CHAPTER 14

MORTA WASN'T ALONE.

There was a black car with darkened windows parked right behind her. Mary gasped, "That's the car that tried to run Kaitlyn off the road!"

The children watched in horror as all four of the car's doors opened and four dark figures emerged. They were tall and brutish looking. They were dressed in worn, black leather. One man was significantly larger than the rest and wore a thick, hooded cape. Morta stepped forward and motioned to the four men to follow her as she crossed the road.

"This is really bad," Christian said, his eyes wide with fear. "They all have demons attached to them, and the biggest guy has even more."

The children closed the front door and scrambled up the stairs. Their parents entered the foyer, carrying the crucifix that had been in the chest. A beam of light shone through one of the thin windows to the side of the door and hit the gold cross. Their mother gasped delightedly as the light reflected off the cross, casting a rainbow hue onto the wall. Shadows within the light projected a series of letters. The family could make out the words, *Tempus est. Nolite timere.*

Liam stood up and cleared his throat, "That's Latin for... "

Mary happily jumped in, "Oh, I've got this! It says: *It is time. Be not afraid.*"

Liam snapped a disapproving look at Mary, who lightly shrugged her shoulders and added, "Sorry, I just couldn't help myself."

Liam sighed and said, "I understand. But I kind of hope your *gift* has an expiration date."

"This is amazing!" their mother cried. "I guess it's time then!"

Their father called up to other children, who were cowering on the steps, "See, you don't have to be afraid, it's time for you to heed the words on the parchment. You must go to Pio's cavern."

Christian had made his way over to a window at the top of the stairs that had a view to the backyard. "We can't go anywhere," he said. "One of the men is already at the back door. I think he's guarding it!"

Allora ran to a side window. "There's one at the side garage door too."

Angelica's eyes widened, "And now they're at the front door as well. We're surrounded!"

"Should we call the police?" Mary asked in a panic.

"No," her father replied, "they won't be defeated in that manner."

Mary was amazed at how her father's words were almost a perfect echo of Padre Pio's.

"Here, take the key," their mother said as she handed it over to Allora. "Is there a place where you can all hide for the time being, until you figure out a way to get into the backyard? Your father and I need to make sure you're safe. We need to carry out our own instructions."

"I know just the place!" Christian called out. "Come on guys! To the new LCAMAS secret meeting place!"

The children hurried up the stairs. Serena hesitated.

"Are you going to be okay?" she asked.

"Don't worry about us," her mother replied. "Just go and hide, and then find a way to make it to the cavern safely."

Morta's men could be heard at the front door, attempting to pick the lock.

Patrick took a deep breath and grabbed his wife's hand.

"Are you ready for this?" he asked. She nodded, and both peered down at the parchment in his hand.

INSTRUCTION #1: GO INTO THE COAT CLOSET.

The couple quickly headed to the closet. It was discretely tucked into the wall under the stairwell.

They waited in perfect silence, as Morta burst into the house with two of her men and barked out instructions. "You two head upstairs and find the children," she commanded, "I'll take care of the parents."

Patrick peered through the crack of the bifold doors. He could see Morta rummaging through her purse. She pulled out a syringe filled with a green, sappy substance and removed the protective cap, revealing its long sharp needle. She walked toward the living room, cautiously holding the needle between her thumb and fingers, calling out, "Hello? It's just me! Are you guys here?" Her voice was a sickeningly sweet falsetto.

Patrick turned to find his wife's eyes had become teary. "What happened to her?" She whispered. Her husband stroked his wife's long, blonde hair.

"I'm sorry," he replied. "I can't imagine how betrayed you

must feel. But for now, we need to focus on getting out of here and making sure our children get to the cavern safely." She nodded and pointed to the second item in the letter:

INSTRUCTION #2: GET THE REMOTE-CONTROLLED CAR AND PROMPTLY EXIT THE HOME.

The couple looked toward the front of the house and noticed the blue toy car only a few feet from the door. "I think this is the first time I'm actually happy Joachim didn't put his toys away," he whispered to his wife. "Let's go."

They crept out of the closet and swiftly collected the toy. They could hear Morta calling out to her men, "They're here somewhere! Find them!"

Patrick slowly opened the door and the couple crept out of the house, almost tripping over a stray cat who was perched on the front porch.

"What are you doing here?" Patrick said, fully annoyed. "Go away."

"She can't," his wife said. "She's instruction #3."

CHAPTER 15

THE CHILDREN RAN DOWN THE HALLWAY INTO the boys' room. They opened the hatch on the closet floor, and one by one they descended the ladder into the small room below. Serena was the last to descend, and she pulled the hatch closed behind her.

"Oh no!" she cried out. "My dress is caught!"

"Just open up the hatch and pull it out," Christian instructed.

"Wait!" Allora called out in a hushed whisper, "I think someone's coming!"

There were a series of muffled voices and noises, and sure enough, the sound of footsteps seemed to be heading in their direction.

"You can't open the hatch now," Liam whispered. "Someone might see it."

"What can I do? I'm stuck," Serena's eyes brimmed with tears and her lip quivered. "I don't want them to catch me."

Allora inspected the dress, "Maybe we can rip your dress to get you free."

Serena sniffed, "But it's my favorite dress."

She sighed and then seemed to resign herself to her dress's sad fate. "Okay, but we need something sharp." The children searched the small area. It was dark and hard to see, but as they felt along the walls, they discovered a few loose nails embedded in the panels. Christian managed to pull one free and used it to puncture a hole in the dress close to the hatch. He ripped the dress and Serena and the rest of the children quietly headed to the other end of the room, as far from the hatch as they could go.

Outside, they could hear furniture being moved around, and the deep, muffled voices seemed to be shouting commands at one another.

"They're going to find us," Liam whispered. "Eventually they'll see the fabric from Serena's dress hanging out and they'll know we're in here. We need to find a way to escape."

There was a loud *SMACK* as the closet door was thrown open. The children winced and drew further away from the hatch.

"Everyone search the walls!" Christian whispered urgently.

"For what?" Liam asked.

"I don't know," Christian replied. "Maybe we'll find something we can use to defend ourselves."

The children frantically felt along the walls, hoping for anything that could be used against the encroaching enemies.

"Over here!" Angelica motioned. "There are a couple of loose boards. I think I can get them out." She pried the two warped panels from the furthest side of the room and soon discovered that she had created a large hole that opened to a gap between the interior and exterior walls of the house.

"Through here!" she whispered excitedly. "Quickly!"

The children began to crawl, one by one, through the opening of the wall. They heard a bellowing voice call out, "There's something here! A hatch in the floor!"

Serena gasped as Christian whisked her through the hole in the wall. Once everyone was accounted for, Christian quickly replaced the two boards, as best as he could, and the children hurried through the dark corridor, away from the intruders.

It was a narrow, dusty passageway, lined with cobwebs. Allora prayed that the cobwebs had long been vacated by their creators.

"Where do we go now?" she whispered.

Liam looked up and noticed a pale stream of light penetrating through the boards above.

"The attic," he said.

He used the framing of the wall to climb up and began to push against the ceiling, searching for a way in.

Liam was spry and surprisingly strong for his lean stature. He propped himself between the two walls and pushed with all his might against one of the attic's worn floorboards. The board readily gave way, and Liam maneuvered his body up through the opening. Once up, he peered down at the others, his face shining with sweat and pride. "I'll see if I can find something to help you all climb up," he said.

Liam was gone, and in a few minutes, the children watched with gratitude as a large emergency rope ladder unraveled down through the opening. They carefully made their way up into the attic.

"It's hot up here," Mary said crinkling her nose.

"We could go back down," Liam teased.

"It's fine," Mary said quickly.

Angelica stepped cautiously over to a window that faced the backyard.

"Now I really wish I could fly," she said, as she peered through the shutters. "Then I could make it to the cavern without the man guarding the back door being able to capture me."

Mary shook her head slowly. "It would take a miracle to get us all there at this point," she said. "Wait a minute! Isn't that your special gift?"

"Yes, but St. Padre Pio said flying wasn't on the list and that's what we'd need to do."

"You should pray for a miracle, Angelica," Mary insisted. "It's worth a shot." Angelica heaved a tired sigh, "All right; I'll give it a go."

She bowed her head and whispered inaudible words, but then stopped and looked up at her siblings. "Prayers are sometimes even more powerful when you pray with others," she said.

"That's right," said Allora. "Scripture says, *'For where two or more gather in my name, there am I with them,'* so maybe we should pray together.»

The children blessed themselves, making the Sign of the Cross. Then Angelica cleared her throat and spoke solemnly, "Lord, we really need you right now. It feels like we're trapped, but we know you can make a way for us. Please help us; stay by our side and show us the way. Amen."

Angelica looked up, and her mouth opened wide in a big, goofy smile.

"Look!" she said, pointing with delight to the side of the window. Hanging outside were several harnesses and cable trolley attachments for a zip line.

"I definitely have never seen those there before. I'd call that a miracle! Maybe we can cross the backyard using a zip line and make it to the cavern before the scary guy down there can get to us."

"It's only a partial miracle," Liam said, "because there's nothing to zip on. We don't have a cable set up, so we're out of luck."

"You don't need luck when you have the gift of miracles," Angelica insisted. "God will make a way; you'll see!"

"What about a clothesline?" Serena asked, as she looked down through the shutters. Liam joined her beside the window.

"Too low," he said. "It's attached to Mom and Dad's bedroom balcony. That's a whole story lower than us."

"But it connects to the tree right beside the clubhouse," Angelica said, "so shouldn't we at least try? Why else would we *miraculously* find these zip line accessories here?"

Angelica surveyed the attic. "Hey!" she said suddenly. "We have the emergency rope ladder! Couldn't we climb down to the balcony and at least try to zip across from there?"

Liam sighed, "We'd have to be extremely quiet, which is almost impossible with all of us kids. Otherwise the man guarding the door will hear us and alert the others."

"We will be *miraculously* quiet."

"Also, it's highly unlikely that the clothesline will be able to handle our weight."

"It will *miraculously* be able to hold our weight."

"But the angle of the line probably isn't steep enough for us to zip across."

"We will zip across... "

"I know, I know... *Miraculously.*"

Angelica giggled, "It seems I may get to fly after all!!!"

The children smiled at their sister's enthusiasm. Christian managed to *quietly* pry the shutters open and hook the ladder onto the ledge of the window. The children tucked the harnesses and cable trolleys under their arms and climbed down to the balcony below. There was a bit of a gap, and Serena almost cried out as she dangled from the ladder, but the older boys helped reel her in and lifted her safely down. They heard voices coming from the bedroom so they stood frozen against the side of the house, away from the sliding doors.

Christian peered around the corner of the wall and saw two figures inside the bedroom, engrossed in an angry dialogue. He dropped to his hands and knees and quickly crawled to the other side of the door. He stood up and motioned for the others to follow suit. The children all crawled, wincing as the wooden structure creaked with every movement.

Once everyone was on the side where the clothesline was secured, they stealthily peered over the edge of the balcony. The man guarding the door to the backyard was pacing back and forth, scanning the area.

"I think we need a diversion," Allora whispered.

Angelica piped up, "Or another *miracle.*"

MEEEEEOOOOOW! It was a panicked shriek that caught everyone's attention. A white cat with orange spots shot around the corner of the house. She was tied to a remote-controlled car and her eyes were wide as she zoomed toward the guard, circling him and veering through his legs.

"WHOA!" he cried out as he temporarily lost his balance. The car and its rider raced back around the corner. The guard stumbled after it.

"I think that was Duchess Thelma," Serena said, giggling.

"Never mind her," Liam whispered, "now's our chance to go!"

He knew their time was limited, so he carefully secured the cable trolleys onto the clothesline and helped tighten the harnesses around his younger siblings. Christian offered to go first, and one by one the children zipped down the line. Angelica stretched out her arms and threw her head back,

"I'M FLYING!" she cried out delightedly.

"Not so loud!" Allora warned. She wasn't certain how long the distraction would detain the man in black.

CHAPTER 16

"LET ME HAVE A TRY," THEIR MOTHER whispered, as the couple crouched behind a thick shrub at the side of their home. Her husband passed her the remote, and both were highly amused at the sight of the spectacle. The cat's eyes bulged in astonishment, as she whirled around in tight circles. The man in pursuit clumsily swung his arms, missing the feline by mere inches.

"WHAT IN THE NAME OF GARFIELD ARE YOU DOING WITH MY CAT???!!!"

Miss Grassy yelled out as she whirled a large purse above her head and became a crazed drone, zeroing in on the assailant. As the purse spiraled, hardcover books shot out, one smacking the man square between the eyes.

Miss Grassy swept up her cat, unwinding a bungee cord that had been holding Duchess Thelma to the toy car. She marched up to the man, her jaw clenched with utter disgust. As he rubbed his forehead, she proceeded to whack him one more time with her large, quilted purse.

"CAT HATER!!!" she cried. The Duchess and Miss Grassy both held their noses in the air and left with a *Hmph!*

The confused man sluggishly headed toward the backyard.

"I hope we gave them enough time to make it to the cavern," the children's father said.

"We definitely gave them a good start," his wife assured him, "and we reunited a wayward cat with her owner." She smiled mischievously... .

"THEY'RE OVER HERE!"

The guard was hot on the children's trail. The injury had not slowed his speed and determination. The children were just nearing the end of the clothesline. They tried not to focus on the brute heading in their direction, as they braced themselves for impact. Christian hit the tree with a thud, as his siblings crashed into him in a series of *"OOOF"*s!

The children's eyes widened as they saw that the man was no longer alone in his pursuit. The rest of Morta's men were racing toward them at great speed.

"Hurry, Allora!" Christian ordered., "We need the key to get into the cavern!"

Allora rushed over to the doors in the ground and hurriedly produced the key. Her hands were shaking, but she managed to fit it into the lock and with a quick turn, the doors dropped open.

"Everyone in!" she called out.

In a frantic scramble, the children descended the staircase.

"WAIT!" Christian called out. "Where's Serena?"

He dashed back up the stairs only to see Serena still dangling from her harness.

"I'm stuck!" she cried out. "Help!"

But it was too late. One of the men swept the little girl up, firmly holding his hand over her mouth. She kicked and squirmed, but he was too strong. In one swift motion, he broke the back section of her necklace, allowing her beautiful cross from Mrs. Berry to fall to the ground.

Christian started toward her, but another one of Morta's men was barreling in his direction and Christian dropped back down into the cavern. The man attempted to thrust himself through the opening after Christian, but with a flash, he was thrown back through the air. He yelped, flapping his arms and legs helplessly as he hit the trunk of a nearby tree and slid down.

Morta's voice cut through the air, "Fool! You can't go into their sacred space."

She arrived at the opening, her face contorted with disdain. The man at the bottom of the tree slowly rose and stumbled toward her, holding his head in pain.

"Wicken, you will remain here and guard the opening," she commanded. "They can't stay in there forever."

Then she abruptly turned and walked away, calling out over her shoulder, "Bring the girl to my car. He'll be happy to have at least acquired one of the little brats."

The children mournfully descended the staircase. Mary let out a wail, as her sisters burst into tears. The boys solemnly stared at each other. Both felt the weight of having failed to protect their little sister.

"I can't believe this is happening," Allora sobbed.

"I'm sorry." The familiar, gruff voice Padre Pio would usually have brought them great joy and comfort, but the children could barely bring themselves to look at the one ascending the staircase.

"You," Christian said accusingly. "If you had been here, our sister would never have been captured. Where were you? Why weren't you here protecting us?"

"I'm here now," he responded softly. "You must believe that in the end, God will have the victory."

"But at what cost?" Allora said, wiping her eyes.

"What will they do to Serena?" Mary asked anxiously. "Will they hurt her... or worse?"

"I'm not sure. It has yet to be revealed to me," the saint replied, "but I do know where they'll be taking her. Liam, I believe you are familiar with the place."

Liam grew pale. "Oh no," he said meekly, "you don't mean..."

"I believe they will be bringing her to the lair of The Devourer."

No one spoke.

"You must go to her. She'll need to be rescued," Padre Pio sighed. "I know that much is being asked of you, but you must find your courage."

"It's just so scary," Allora admitted. "We don't know what will be waiting for us."

"We know our sister will be waiting for us," Liam said solemnly.

Allora smiled, remembering her little sister's example of bravery. "That's true," she said, "so it doesn't matter what else we might find."

"But how will we get there? Morta has a guard posted at the entryway," Angelica asked. Then she had a thought. "Oooooh, can we bilocate there? That would be so cool!"

"I'm sorry, my dear," the saint said. "No bilocating this time. We'll need your full attention, so it's probably better to remain in one location at a time."

"Hey, if you were bilocating and one of your bodies was injured or killed, would the other be wounded or fall down dead too?" Christian asked with wide eyes.

Padre Pio stared at the boy. "I've never pondered that question... I don't know... and quite honestly, I don't think I'd want to find out."

"Well, then how are we going to get past the guard at the

entryway?" Allora asked.

"Ah! You assume it is the *only* entryway, but it is not so," St. Pio said, raising an eyebrow. "Follow me."

CHAPTER 17

THE CHILDREN FOLLOWED THE SAINT. THEY ventured through the dark tunnel until they came to the chamber where they had first encountered Padre Pio.

"There," he pointed to something wooden in the room's furthest corner. It resembled a large, ornate wardrobe. "In there."

Angelica cried out in excitement, "Is that a porthole to another dimension?!"

"No," the saint replied. "Armor. We are going into battle."

"YES!" Christian exclaimed. "It's about time!"

The doors to the cabinet had an inscription in Latin.

"Let me guess," Liam huffed. "Mary will translate."

"You can do it, Liam," Mary said. "I don't mind."

Liam smiled and shifted his glasses. "It's Latin for: *Put on the armor of God and take your stand against the evil one."*

Padre Pio was at his side. "Actually, this time you'll find power in the words when pronounced in their original tongue."

The boy looked intently at the saint, who smiled warmly. Liam cleared his throat and called out in a voice that was deep and powerful, *"Induite vos armaturam Dei stare adversus malignum."*

The cabinet throbbed and glowed with the same intensity as when the cavern was first discovered. The two wooden doors burst open, and everyone gasped in amazement as a great light burst forth.

"WHOA!"

The intense bluish streams broke into fragments that formed shapes and figures, dancing, dueling, and forging great battles. The children recognized various saints whose stories had been recounted to them from the time they were babies. These heroes had waged wars against the darkness and won many souls for Christ.

"I see St. Joan of Arc!" Angelica said excitedly. The figure of a young woman with short hair, bearing a sword and raising a banner, danced through the air. She twirled and clashed her sword against her enemy, who was not quite a soldier, but a twisted dark figure. "She's so amazing,» Angelica sighed.

"Hey!" Allora cried out. "That's you! It's *your* story!" She looked at Padre Pio with delight as she pointed to a bluish figure of a man. The children watched in awe as he held what looked like a simple rosary, which then transformed into a great chain. A dragon reared its head, flares of fire shooting from its throat again and again. With each hit, a great shield became visible, protecting the figure from the force of the flames. It seemed to absorb and dispel the fire before disappearing altogether. The man lassoed the chain around the monster's neck. It was almost electric in nature, choking the beast and bringing it to its knees.

Padre Pio reached out his hand, waving it through the luminescent figures. They swirled like whispery smoke before vanishing. "You, too, will bring this evil to its knees," he said, his eyes twinkling. "If only you could understand how dear you are to the Father, you would have faith in his ability to protect you and to lead you to victory."

The cabinet was filled with armor that seemed to be made of the same bluish light as the figures that had been released. Christian approached them with awe and wonder, reaching his hand out to touch them. His hand glided through each item, revealing them all to be merely swirling clouds of light.

"These are just holograms! They're not real at all." He looked disappointedly at the saint. "We can't even wear them, and even if we could, I don't think they would protect us from anything."

"You are blessed that they are being made visible to you," Padre Pio replied. "Most people cannot see what you view before you here, although these pieces of armor exist at all times in the *real* world. They are comprised of the graces and virtues that equip mankind to face that force whose only desire is to extinguish Christ's brilliant light and to separate you from the Father's love."

He patted the boy on the back. "Now stand back, all of you. Spread out your arms and suit up!"

The children obeyed, their eyes curiously darting back and forth.

"The sacrifices you've made, the virtues you've exhibited... all these have brightened the light within you. They've set you apart; they've helped preserve you from the darkness. Now you will see the wondrous way Our Lord protects his children. You will be putting on the full armor of God."

The saint's voice rang out as the cabinet almost groaned from the intensity of the light within.

"Your feet have been prepared with the Gospel of Peace. These boots will carry you swiftly to your destination, and just as you stand confidently in the assurance of God's Word, you will stand firm against the enemy."

Just then, several pairs of holographic boots flew from the cabinet and circled the children.

SWOOSH, FLUMP! The children were thrown back from the impact as the lustrous footwear enveloped their feet.

Next, the cabinet released what looked like ribbons of the bluish light that danced around the children. Angelica giggled as one of the pieces swirled around her head, then neck, and wrapped itself around her waist, cinctured with a glistening clasp.

"The belt of truth! You will not be easily ensnared by the darkness, my dear children, as you have heard the truth of the Gospel and *the truth will always set you free!*"

Soon, five large pieces of armor rose before them, hovering in the air. "The Breastplates of Righteousness! You, my children, are so dear to the Father and, as you have entrusted your very lives to him, so shall he assure that you are all protected. These breastplates will not allow the force of evil to penetrate your hearts, for your hearts belong to God alone!"

In one swift motion, the armor clamped itself onto each child.

"It feels like a big hug!" cried Mary.

"When your heart is right with God, it *is* like a big hug," the saint laughed. "His love is also like a shield about you, protecting you from every angle."

"Like a force field?" Liam asked. "Because that would be very helpful in the exigency of the moment."

Padre Pio stared at the boy for a moment. "I must admit, sometimes I find it difficult to decipher your use of the English language. *Force field?*"

"You're not the only one," Angelica asserted. "*Exigency?* Really, Liam?"

The saint chuckled, "Well, if a force field is anything like the Shield of Faith, then yes! You will be well equipped!"

"Where are the shields?" Angelica asked, scanning the room. "I don't see them."

"They will appear just as they did in the unfolding stories of the saints before you. When the evil forces spew fiery darts and lashes of fire, your shield will be made visible and will absorb every blow."

"And now, a favorite of mine: the Helmets of Salvation!"

The helmets were majestic and radiant. They floated toward the children, slowly lowering down upon their heads. The air was thick with wonder and excitement, as though it were a coronation. Padre Pio spoke with fervency, "Nothing will sway you from your goal when your mind is set on God. These helmets will help keep you focused on your task and will not allow dark thoughts to lead you astray."

"Plus, they look really cool too!" Christian couldn't help adding.

"I think you'll find the next item to your liking, or *cool,* as you say," said the saint, smiling.

"Behold the swords of the Spirit, which is the Word of God!"

The room was filled with the clinking and clanking of clashing swords. They shot forth from the cabinet, animated and dueling one another, flying about the room seemingly intent on impressing the children below, who smiled and squealed at the display. Mary clapped her hands and called out, "Amazing!" The swords ceased battling and seemed to stand at attention before leaning in and taking a bow.

"All other pieces of armor serve to protect and defend you, but with the Word of God, which cuts through the lies and confusion, you will be a force to be reckoned with. You will drive back the evil that encroaches upon you. You will battle the darkness."

"Not to seem ungrateful," Allora spoke up, "but I've always wanted to try out archery."

The saint thought for a moment. "Hmmmm, yes. I think that could be arranged." He turned to one of the swords. "Would you mind terribly?"

The sword began to spin. It picked up speed, spinning faster and faster until it became a blurry ball of light. When it came to a halt, the children gasped delightedly at its transformation. The sword was now a bow, complete with a quiver of arrows, and it gracefully glided down to Allora. She clasped it in awe. Two more of the swords began to spin and when they stopped, the children saw they had been transformed into a crossbow and twin daggers. The crossbow darted toward Mary, and the daggers found a home in Angelica's belt. The girls looked at one another excitedly.

The boys reached out their hands, and the remaining swords flew swiftly to them. They were double edged and magnificent to behold. Both Christian and Liam were speechless as they sliced the air with the brilliant blades.

"One more thing," Padre Pio said as he made his way to the cabinet. He entered it and emerged promptly, his arms draped with colorful fabrics. "My gift to you!" he said smiling. "You said yes to placing yourselves in God's service, and for your courageous offering, I have asked the Father for a special favor. Behold the Cloaks of Zeal."

He began to pass out the hooded cloaks to the children. They were each a distinct color and pattern. Liam's was a dark, regal blue; Christian's, a velvety red; Allora's was a suede, luxurious purple; Mary's, a satiny cloak covered in teal swirls; and Angelica's was a creamy, sunny yellow that became iridescent when she twirled.

"LOVE, LOVE, LOVE them!!!" Mary squealed.

"Oh and just so you're aware," the saint added, "they just might be invisibility cloaks."

"WHAT??" Christian had found his voice. "How do they work?" He fiddled around with the fabric, looking for a button or *on* switch. Just then he felt something pinch his nose, followed by a trilling giggle. Angelica seemed to appear out of nowhere. Her hands were clenching the hood of the cape.

"The hoods!" she said, her eyes sparkling. "Put on your hood and disappear! It's so fun!"

She demonstrated with a shrill of laughter. POOF! She vanished.

"Ah, but they don't make your voice or giggles disappear," Padre Pio said as he found her hood and pulled it back, causing the little girl to reappear. "So you'll have to exhibit a little bit of self-mastery."

He stepped back and surveyed the group, resplendent in their shimmery, rich cloaks and encircled in the lustrous, translucent glow of armor. They were indeed a marvel to be seen.

The saint appeared satisfied. "We're ready."

CHAPTER 18

"SO HOW DO WE GET THERE?" ALLORA ASKED, scanning the walls.

St. Pio crossed the room toward the fireplace. The fire was blazing, but as the saint reached out and pulled on a statue half-embedded above the hearth, the flame disappeared. The sound of gears grinding and clicking could be heard as the stones inside the fireplace, from the floor up to just beneath the mantle, began to separate. The two halves slid apart, revealing a tunnel behind.

"Oh, I LOVE secret passageways!" Mary cried out.

"Come!" the saint said briskly. "We should hurry."

He ducked his head and proceeded through the opening. The children followed. Allora glanced up at the statue that had opened the secret door. She smiled, as she recognized the figure: St. Nicholas Owen, who had built secret rooms and hideouts for priests during their persecution in England long ago. How appropriate, she thought, as she lowered her head and passed through to the tunnel beyond.

Padre Pio stood staring down the long corridor. FLIFT, FLIFT, FLIFT, FLIFT. One by one, torches lining the sides of the tunnel ignited, revealing the vast distance ahead. A series of doors, a spectrum of colors, were on either side.

Liam squinted his eyes, peering into what seemed to be an abyss of light. "I can't see the end. How far does it go?"

The saint turned to the children. "It's very far, indeed," he said, "but I think you're going to like this next phase of our journey!"

Angelica frowned and stood with her hands on her hips. "I have short legs. I'm not really liking the idea of walking a gazillion miles! Is there any chance of revisiting the flying option?"

Padre Pio raised an eyebrow. "And miss out on the opportunity to test out your new footwear? Not a chance! It is a great distance, but I think you'll find it's one you're more than well equipped to handle." He beamed. "Now, run!"

Christian was the first to respond, and as he began to dash, he couldn't believe what was happening. Each stride covered at least ten of his usual steps. The ground beneath him seemed to roll as his feet grazed the surface, shooting him ahead. He stopped suddenly and looked back for the others. He was shocked to discover that in only a few steps, he was already about half a mile down the tunnel. In a moment, the others caught up to him. They were all alive with excitement and surprise at their newly acquired speed.

"I LOVE THIS!" Angelica exclaimed, "I'm not even tired. Will I get tired?" She turned, asking Padre Pio, who had remained at their side.

"No," he answered, "you have shod your feet with the preparation of the Gospel of Peace. You will remain at peace, even as you travel great distances!"

"Awesome!" she cried out as she returned to her flight. The children laughed and joined her. It was a strange sensation, to be running without the slightest breath, effortlessly thrusting ahead, the stone walls and colorful doors blurred from the pace and the torches but a streak of light.

The children could have run forever, but they heard Padre Pio call out, "Stop!"

It was a bit difficult, but they managed to slide to a halt. Christian let out a disappointed, "AWWW! That was incredible! I wish we could keep going!"

"We're here. There's a red door to your left, but first I will consult... "

The saint's voice trailed off as he looked sharply above the doorway, "My dear friend! What are you doing here? Why aren't you guarding your child? It's not safe to leave him. Oh... oh no... I see. Oh dear."

The old man's face grew dim, and he turned back to the children, his eyes filled with deep concern and sadness. "It would seem that your little sister is not the only one who's been captured."

"No!" Allora gasped, "Who else have they taken?"

"That was your brother Joachim's guardian angel."

He paused for a moment and took a deep breath. "They have your cousin and... " he hesitated. "They have your little siblings."

"Which ones?" Allora asked, her breath short and weak.

"All of them."

Allora closed her eyes and lowered her head. It was too painful to think of her sweet little siblings in the hands of the dark figures.

Mary's eyes welled up with tears, "Poor babies!" she cried. "They must be so scared and confused."

Angelica's chin was stiff, her temper fuming. "How dare they!!! Let me at 'em!!!" She ran to the door, determined to burst through. The saint caught her around the waist and whisked her back to the far side of the passageway.

"No, child, not yet," he said, bending down to meet her eyes. "If we are to rescue your siblings, we must devise a plan. Your foe will not easily be overcome, and we should proceed with caution, knowing that there are many little innocent lives counting on us."

He placed his hand gently on her head. "Peace, Little One. All will be well. Do not forget, we already know who has the victory."

Angelica took a deep breath. "Just tell us what to do."

CHAPTER 19

THE LAIR WAS FILLED WITH THE WHIMPERING of little voices. It was dark save for a few dim torches on the walls, their flames an eerie shade of red. The prisoners were being kept in a cage about the size of a large shed. Kaitlyn held the youngest close, whispering, "It's going to be okay, Baby Girl." It was partly in an effort to reassure herself. The infant curled up under Kaitlyn's neck, seemingly oblivious to the dark forces surrounding her.

It was all so surreal. After leaving her aunt's home, Kaitlyn had stopped at a local park. Her brothers were excited to see their little cousins at first, but after pushing them on the swings for what felt like an eternity, lifting Joa up to the monkey bars for the trillionth time, and attempting to stop the twins from throwing sand pies... or eating them, they had had their fill. They helped Kaitlyn chase down and load up the rambunctious tots.

"We'll see you at home, Kaitlyn," her brother Michael called out. "We'll tell Mom you're coming."

"And that she should tie up the cupboards and toilets!" her brother Daniel added.

"See you there," Kaitlyn replied. "I'm just going to stop for some gas first."

Once she was on her way, Kaitlyn turned down the same road where she had lost control just earlier that day. The memory of the black car that had tried to run her off the road made her shudder.

"What is wrong with people?" she thought out loud. "I hope I never see that car again." Then the loud revving of an engine made her jump. She glanced at her rearview mirror and froze in terror as she caught sight of the very same car swerving and squealing just behind her. She gasped.

"No," she whispered, "not again."

Panic stricken, she sped up, but then faltered in her determination. *What if I can't stop again? What will happen to the littles?* The black car pulled up beside her and then cut in front of her. Her foot pressed hard on the brakes, bring the van to a screeching halt. Kaitlyn fumbled for the lock button, but before she could hit it, a man was at her side window. He ripped the door open and thrust a rag saturated with some type of chemical over the bottom half of her face. She fought to pry his hands off, but he was too strong and the fumes from the cloth were making her dizzy. Everything blurred around her as she lost consciousness. When she woke, she had an immense headache, which was fueled by the strange musty odor that filled the lair.

"I no like it here," Kiara peeped. «We go home now."

Joachim piped up, "Dis place smells like scary!"

Kaitlyn bent down to comfort her little cousin. She put her arm around him, saying, "We'll figure out a way to get home soon."

She looked out through the black iron bars and could make out four figures arguing at a distance. One, a man wearing a black, hooded cape, was carrying a sack with some type of animal inside, wriggling and squealing. Kaitlyn gasped as he turned abruptly and headed her way.

"Come here everyone!" she said, motioning the little ones to the far side of the cage. She stood in front of them, extending her free arm as a shield separating them from the dark figure approaching them, the sack slumped over his shoulder.

"LET ME OUT OF HERE!"

Kaitlyn jumped at the sound of the screeching voice coming from the sack.

"QUIET BRAT!" said the dark-caped man. Kaitlyn soon heard the loud clinking and jingling of keys, as the man struggled to brace the sack while opening the door to the cage. Once opened, he tossed the sack inside before slamming it closed again.

"OWW!" the sack complained. Kaitlyn laid Baby Callie down in a pile of straw in the corner of the cell and rushed over to untie the laces. She was surprised to see her little cousin emerge, her hair tousled and her face red with fury.

"Ugh! How dare you!" Serena looked at Kaitlyn and her anger quickly turned to relief, "Kaitlyn! I'm so glad to see you!" She buried her face in her cousin's shoulder.

Kaitlyn hugged her and tried to comfort the little girl, who was clearly worn from the traumatic experience.

"What are you doing here?" her muffled voice was scarcely audible. "We were taken from the van just down the road from your house."

"We?" Serena asked as she pulled away from her cousin. Then she noticed the other occupants of the cage.

"Oh no! They captured *all* the littles? This is terrible!"

"Do you know what they want from us?" Kaitlyn asked. Serena shook her head.

"Whatever it is, it can't be good."

The clicking of heels echoed throughout the lair.

"I think that's Morta," Serena whispered. "She's headed our way. That horrid woman is not getting her hands on any of the littles." She ran to the baby who was sweetly cooing in the straw and picked her up, holding her tightly to her chest.

"It's no use," Morta's voice rang out. "You can't protect them. You can't even protect yourself."

"Stay back!" Serena called out. "I'm warning you!"

Morta laughed. "Your friend's not here to help you this time. You are in The Devourer's lair now and it seems... oh how sad, you've misplaced your little necklace. Not to worry though, I have one to replace it."

"I won't wear your evil necklace! You can't make me!"

"I love your feisty spirit, but trust me, my dear, your flesh is very weak."

"You better leave us all alone, or I'm gonna call my Mother!" Serena threatened.

Morta threw her head back, releasing a maniacal, arrogant shrill of laugher.

"Your mother is far away, and I think you'll discover that she in no match for the master."

Serena narrowed her eyes. She spoke slowly, her voice ripe with determination. "I wasn't talking about *that* mother."

Morta's smug smile disappeared. She stepped back and, for a moment, Serena could detect fear in her eyes.

"Deviron!" Morta called out. "Come here!"

The hooded man approached Morta. She pointed a long, spindly finger toward the infant in Serena's arms. "Bring me the baby."

Serena slowly backed away as the large, menacing figure unlocked the gate once again and advanced toward her and the small infant. He raised his hands; they were large, chapped, a deathly grey. The baby girl turned her head toward him and smiled through her coos. Serena thought she saw a flare of light extending from her baby sister.

Deviron jumped back, startled. He shot an accusing look at Morta and growled, "Freshly baptized."

"UUUUUGH!" Morta said in an exasperated moan. "Why does EVERYTHING have to be so complicated with you little maggots?!"

"Leave her alone! She's just a baby!" Kaitlyn cried out to the display of evil standing before her. "What's wrong with you?? Why are you doing this? Just let us go!"

Morta eyed the teenager carefully. "We weren't expecting you," she snapped. She tilted her head slightly, as though she were devising a new plan. "But... you may prove useful. Take her!" she ordered the henchman. Kaitlyn knew she was no match for Deviron and so raised her hands in surrender. "I'll go with you, but only if you leave the others alone." She left the cage, her eyes pleading with Morta. "Where is your heart?"

Morta turned on her heel and briskly walked away toward a winding tunnel. She called out to Deviron over her shoulder, "Take the girl to the Chamber of Ansmacht for her procedure! I'll meet you there shortly."

Morta turned a corner and pressed her back against the stone wall. She took a deep breath and

snapped, "Get it together!"

She never liked being in the presence of babies. They reminded her of Lily... and Lily was no longer hers. She was simply a dream that had ended before it had really begun.

"It's better this way. No regrets," she assured herself.

The one she answered to promised empowerment and freedom if she would leave Lily behind, and now The Devourer would help her forget the pain. He promised he would. He promised everything would be better this way.

CHAPTER 20

"WHAT'S OUR PLAN?" ANGELICA STARED intently at St. Pio.

"We will need some assistance from our angelic friends. They will help us understand the scope of what we're up against."

Mary looked confused. "If Kaitlyn and the littles have their guardian angels close by, why can't their angels just swoop down and save them?"

"We may not always understand the Father's plan, but we can trust he has his reasons for allowing things to unfold this way."

"But there's so much at stake. I wish God would just fix everything."

"He will."

"Do Morta and the bad guys have guardian angels too?"

"They do, but their angels respect the gift of free will that has been given to each soul, so they will not act unless the one entrusted to their care desires their assistance... and as it stands, Morta and her associates are held fast by fallen angels who will not readily release their grip."

Christian surveyed the hallway. There were so many doors!

"Where do all these doors lead?" he asked. He tried a few of the knobs, but they were locked.

"These doors remain closed to those who are not meant to enter," the saint said gently, redirecting Christian back to the red door.

Padre Pio looked up suddenly, once again conversing with a hidden informant.

"Lead the way, Dear Friend," he said, before turning to the children. "It's time," he told them with a firm voice. "Be brave and know that Our Lord accompanies us. Hoods up, and do not speak a word. Our enemy may send a soldier to inspect the tunnel at any time. Your footwear will ensure that your steps are shrouded in silence. The shields about you will hide any trace of your spiritual light from The Devourer's keen senses, but still, you must remain vigilant."

He turned back to the door, closed his eyes, and lowered his head. The saint extended his hand, as though he were performing a solemn blessing. His lips moved quickly, pouring out an inaudible prayer. Then, he marked the Sign of the Cross on the door and brought his hand to the knob, turning it ever so slowly. The door was a silent friend, refusing to draw attention to their arrival. It opened to a long tunnel, similar to the one Liam had ventured through when Padre Pio had first brought him to the lair, but it was much darker, and not sloped.

The saint pulled his hood over his head and vanished from sight. The children wondered how they would be able to follow someone they couldn't see, but there was a small flickering light toward the ceiling, and they somehow knew that they had an additional guide. They started moving cautiously through the tunnel. Mary moved a little too quickly and bumped into Allora.

"Oooof, sorry," she whispered, "I just can't see or hear anyone."

"Let's all hold hands," Allora whispered back.

"Good idea," Christian added. He was in the lead and reached out to find the hand of Angelica, who was right behind him. She held Allora's hand; Allora grasped onto Mary's hand, and Mary found Liam's. Liam was determined to take up the rear and ensure no enemies would catch them by surprise from behind. He also thought it would also make for an expeditious retreat... only if necessary, of course. They hesitantly proceeded toward the lair.

Suddenly, they heard the sound of loud, heavy footsteps echoing through the tunnel. They saw the cast of an orange glow against the wall, as one of Morta's henchmen rounded the corner, clenching a torch. His walk was determined and menacing and the children were greatly relieved to be hidden from his view. But still, they pressed their backs against the stone wall and held their breath. The brute stopped short and surveyed the area, tilting his head as he glared down the darkened path. He seemed satisfied that the tunnel was secure and started back toward the lair.

Just then he stumbled. He turned around sharply, thoroughly inspecting the ground. He shook his head in confusion.

Christian slowly drew his foot back in, chastising himself not having been more cautious. The man shot his hand out, still grasping the torch onto the side of the tunnel and missing Mary's head by a mere inch. She tensed her face, as the flame roared just above her. She turned her head slowly away from the villain. He was so close she could feel the heat of the flame and smell the sweat rolling down the villain's face.

He leaned against the wall and adjusted his shoe. The back had come off when he'd stumbled. He made the adjustment and then stood tall once more. He surveyed the area, looking perturbed, sniffing and wiping the back of his hand across his brow.

The children were tense with fear. Could he sense their presence?

Finally, he shrugged his shoulders and ventured back from whence he came.

They waited a few minutes. His footsteps could be heard

off in the distance. "I think it's safe to continue," Padre Pio whispered. "Remember: vigilance. Onward."

They moved more swiftly now, in perfect silence. All marveled at how their footsteps left no imprint on the soft dirt floor, no trace or evidence of their journey. They soon felt a swell of heat rolling into the tunnel and winced at the red glow ahead. The mouth of the lair was lined with an eruption of sharp, jagged rocks, a ferocious jaw warning them not to enter.

The light, which had so faithfully led them, vanished. Padre Pio suddenly appeared, as he pulled back his hood, and spoke. "Our first priority is to free your youngest siblings."

He crouched behind the shards of rock at the entrance, peering through the archway. The tunnel had brought them to the end of a large, dark pit. A ledge no more than two feet wide circled the pit. They saw the henchman who had recently emerged from their tunnel. He was slowly walking the path, making his way to a hanging bridge.

He muttered under his breath, "I hate this thing..." He stepped onto the thin, brittle bridge, holding on firmly to the twined rails. The bridge swayed and creaked. Every few steps a board shifted slightly, throwing the large man off balance.

When he finally made it to the other side, he exhaled and approached the iron cage against the far wall. The small children were yelling and whining. He banged on the rails,

THE DEVOURER'S LAIR

calling out, "Quiet! You don't want to get our master angry, now do you? Personally, I think we should just throw you all into the pit."

The voices relented and turned to soft whimpers and muted sniffles. The man continued on his way.

"We must get the little ones to safety before we engage the enemy," Padre Pio said. "Christian and Allora, I'm tasking you with the mission of rescuing your siblings. Don't use the bridge. It is frequently inspected and though your footwear would hide the sound of your steps, the bridge would sway and alert the enemy to your presence. You will take the path in the other direction, all the way to the edge of the lair. There is a sliver of a ledge that lines the western rim. It is dangerously thin—at most, half a foot's width—but your footwear is sound and your guardian angels have assured me that they will be close at hand to assist you. Still, you must be careful, for a fall into the pit is a plunge into the very heart of darkness."

Allora took a deep breath and tried to summon her courage.

"Do we need a key," Christian inquired, "for when we arrive at the cage?"

"Your sword will suffice, but again you must use caution. We don't want the noise to draw any attention. Keep your hoods up until you reach the cage."

"Everyone else, stay close to me." Padre Pio lifted his gaze above them. "Where did you say they're taking the children's cousin?" He paused for a moment. "Ah yes, I thought as much. We will need to stop that procedure."

CHAPTER 21

"STOP DRAGGING YOUR FEET!" KAITLYN'S assailant shoved her from behind. Kaitlyn pressed her lips together and stared at the dark, dusty path beneath her Converse boots. She was determined to continue her sluggish pace no matter how hard he pushed her. She was in no hurry to get to their destination.

Just ahead, she saw a cave-like structure. An illusory, green glow lit it from within. She felt nauseous and panic-stricken all at once. "Please don't take me in there," she pleaded.

She recognized the cruel clicking of heels behind her. "Deviron! Bring her in." Morta walked brusquely ahead of them.

The Chamber was large and ominous, with a much higher ceiling than Kaitlyn expected. Through the darkness she could see tiny flashes of red and blackened ripples of motion, leading her to believe the chamber was ripe with unfriendly beings.

A large table presided in the center of the room. Beside it sat a large, sinister-looking chair. It was made of thick slabs of wood and covered in a series of leather belts and restraints.

"We can do this one of two ways," Morta mused, her voice coy and taunting, "the painful way, or the even *more* painful way."

"How about neither," Kaitlyn shot back.

Morta walked to the far side of the chamber and lifted a large trunk from a cabinet embedded in the wall. She brought it to the table and slowly opened it. It was eerily musical, a sickening siren, the whistling and clinking clamor of crystals. The green light they emitted was fully unsettling. Kaitlyn found that her entire body was repulsed by the formations.

Morta pulled out a single crystal before shutting the lid. She opened a small drawer hidden in the table and produced a mortar and pestle. She smacked the crystal with the stone pestle and broke it in two, placing half of the green gem in the mortar and setting the other aside. With great effort she ground the crystal with the pestle, until the shard became a fine, gritty powder.

"Deviron! Wine!" Morta held out her hand expectantly, as Deviron rushed to the cabinet and pulled out a large jug and a clay goblet. He set them on the table with a loud thud. Morta looked at him sideways, fully annoyed. "Pour it, Fool!"

He frowned and snarled but granted her request, handing her the goblet, half full of the red liquid. She took the mortar and scraped the contents into the wine, stirring it briskly with the pestle. "I hope you're thirsty," she said to Kaitlyn, "because your cooperation will mean the experience will be less painful. It will go down easily enough, but I don't envy the storm it will create in your stomach. It has a certain possessive quality in that it will travel throughout your body and take hold of every cell, every muscle." She smiled and looked squarely at her captive. "Your body will no longer be your own. Even as you fight to regain control, your effort will be in vain. You will serve The Devourer."

She walked toward Kaitlyn, her hands caressing the goblet. Kaitlyn turned her face away in disgust. "Thanks, but no thanks."

"I strongly advise you to reconsider," Morta threatened.

Kaitlyn sighed. "Fine," she said, the word bitter in her mouth. She tentatively took the goblet and slowly brought it to her lips.

In a flash of spite, she whipped the goblet across the room, calling out, "Never!" It smashed into pieces against the wall, leaving a crimson smear, which was her glaring mark of defiance.

"Hmmmn," Morta shrugged lightly, "I'm not surprised. I assumed you would choose the hard way."

Kaitlyn slowly backed away from her captors. "You think I'm afraid? Do your best!" she said, her jaw still tight with resolve.

"The *more* painful way it is!" Morta said callously. Two of Morta's men appeared behind Kaitlyn. They were identical twin brothers. One locked his stone-like arms around her, while she kicked and wriggled, trying to escape his grip.

"Skullen, Scaylen, strap her in!" Morta ordered. "Drinking it amiably would have been much nicer for you. You see, Deviron can get a little rough when he forces our guests to consume our special serum. He once dislocated a poor man's jaw in the process!"

Kaitlyn winced.

Skullen dragged Kaitlyn over to the wooden chair, clamping her in place, while Scaylen tightly strapped her wrists and ankles. Morta walked over to the small drawer once more and pulled out a small glass. Kaitlyn squirmed in her seat, desperately trying to pry her hands free of the restraints.

"I don't understand. You have enough men to help you with your horrible, evil plans. Why do you need me?"

"Simple. The Devourer is most pleased with the demise of the innocent... and unfortunately we're prevented from bringing a certain innocent member of your extended family to my boss, due to our... dedicated allegiance. But you can take on the task for us. You, acting as an unwilling servant, will be able to bring the baby to The Devourer. You'll have no choice."

"Not going to happen!" Kaitlyn insisted fervently. "There's no way I'd ever let you touch that baby!"

"We shall see," Morta sneered. "You'll have to excuse me for a moment while I prepare the serum." And with that she turned back to the the table and began grinding the other half of the crystal.

CHAPTER 22

"LET'S GO," CHRISTIAN WHISPERED. Allora grabbed onto her brother's cape and followed behind him as he made his way along the path toward the western rim. About a hundred feet away, they caught sight of the the thin ledge over the blackened pit.

"He wasn't kidding," Christian whispered. "It's so thin, I don't know how we're going to make it across without falling."

"I know we'll be fine. It's like in my mind, I can already see us on the other side," Allora said softly. "Maybe it's my gift... at least I hope it is, 'cause then we can trust that everything will be okay."

"I hope so too," her brother sighed, "'cause it's a long way down."

They hesitantly approached the jagged lip and began to slide their feet along the path. They hugged the stone wall, unwilling to look down into the blackness below. Their pace was slow and methodical. About halfway across the divide, Christian felt the rocky surface beginning to swell, the wall projecting beyond the thin ledge beneath his feet. His sense of balance was faltering.

"We can't go any further," Christian said, frozen in place. "There's no way."

"There has to be," Allora whispered. "I saw it."

"We have to go back, or we'll both... " Christian stopped short, gasping. It was as though unseen hands were cradling his back.

"It can't be," he said incredulously. "He said our angels would be here... but is this for real?"

In a moment of faith and wonder, he let go of the wall, allowing the full weight of his body to fall into the steadfast grip of the angelic presence. His feet remained on the slivery path, but his body hung at an angle, hovering above the pit. He shuffled his feet, barely touching the ledge, and easily floated under the wall's bouldered protrusions.

"Where are you?" Allora whispered urgently, still attempting to scale the wall. Christian had forgotten that he was still invisible.

"Allora, let go of the wall and lean back," he instructed.

"WHAT?!" It was hard for her to keep her voice down, "Are you crazy?"

"Just do it," he replied. "Just trust and know that you are in God's hands."

Allora took a deep breath and slowly let go of the wall. She soon felt the warmth of a presence behind her and leaned back into its heavenly embrace. "Amazing," she said, bathed in astonishment. She felt as though she were flying.

The two children moved swiftly along the remainder of the path. Once they reached the landing, they felt the hands gently pushing them upright and onward, nudging them in the direction of their imprisoned siblings.

"Thank you," Allora whispered to her unseen companion.

"Poor Angelica," she sighed, "she's going to be so jealous."

Allora's angel left the girl. Padre Pio had tasked him with keeping the saint abreast of their progress. He found the troupe moving slowly along the path toward the other end of the lair, and related the news that the children had successfully crossed over the pit.

St. Pio nodded silently and waved, encouraging the angel to return to his ward.

The path was ending and the saint knew that they were nearing the tunnel to the Chamber. There was a large cave ahead.

Padre Pio whispered, "Be extra careful here. The path is dangerously sloped toward the pit."

He found Angelica's hand and cautiously led the train of children toward the cave. Just then, he heard an urgent squeal and Mary suddenly appeared, her hood having fallen back as she slid toward the dark void.

"Ahh! Liam, Help!" Liam grabbed her arms and struggled to pull her back up onto the pathway.

"Are you okay?" he asked in a hushed whisper.

Mary stood up trembling and dusted off her cloak, "Yeah," she sighed, "I was kind of daydreaming."

"In here?" Liam whispered, fully surprised at the idea.

Mary smiled, looking a little embarrassed. "Uh huh."

Liam shook his head. "You need to tighten your helmet," he said.

The children hurried into the cave, and St. Pio pulled back his hood. "We're almost at the Chamber of Ansmacht. It's where they've taken your cousin."

"Ansmacht?" Angelica asked, "What does that mean?"

"Oppression," Mary replied sadly, "and I don't like the sound of that."

"The enemy wants to enslave the human race, to lead us away from God's love, that we might become his prisoners, held fast in the bondage of our sin. He has ensnared Morta and her men, but his appetite is insatiable. His eyes are set on the innocent. He would love nothing more than to have you and your young siblings offered to him. His hold is strong, thus he will not be easily defeated. I tell you this not to scare you, but to help you understand the enormity of what we're up against."

The children were solemnly quiet as the saint continued, "The Eastern Tunnel is at the far end of this cave and leads directly to the chamber. Liam, you will be joining me in attempting to rescue your cousin. Mary and Angelica, you have a big task at hand and it will require all the courage you can muster..."

"Oh dear," Angelica sighed.

"And perhaps a bit of theatrics too," the saint added.

Mary perked up, "Hmm?"

CHAPTER 23

D**EVIRON WAS IMPATIENT. "I THOUGHT YOU** already prepared some of that serum for a syringe earlier," he muttered.

"I did," she huffed, "but I'm saving that particular dose for someone else."

She turned to Kaitlyn, singing out, "Almost ready!" She poured the serum into the small glass and stirred it with a few ounces of water. "I could put your dose into a syringe too and simply stick you with a needle, but I think Deviron actually enjoys it when he gets to... encourage our guests to consume it." Kaitlyn lowered her head and prayed, "God, please help me."

"Oh, don't do that," Morta's tone was deadly flat. "Your prayers won't penetrate these walls... and even if they did, I think you'd find they'd fall on deaf ears. You think God cares about you? Don't kid yourself. He may have set the world into motion, but like an entitled, self-absorbed toddler, he merely batted his toy and then stepped back, distancing himself from the aftermath. Believe me. You are alone."

Morta's face was inches from her young prisoner's. She looked worn, stripped of hope, depleted of life.

Kaitlyn looked deep into her assailant eyes. "I feel sorry for you," she said softly.

Morta's face twitched, but only momentarily, before slowly raising her hand, prominently displaying the small glass. She tauntingly stroked Kaitlyn's cheek. "I feel *more* sorry for *you*."

Deviron clenched the girl's face from behind, forcing open her jaw. Kaitlyn fought in vain to close her mouth and turn away, but Morta swiftly poured the contents of the glass into her mouth. Deviron forced her mouth closed and Morta pressed her hand over Kaitlyn's nose. "Swallow, please, or you'll suffocate," she commanded, as the struggling teenager wrangled and twisted her body fighting for air. Kaitlyn couldn't hold out any longer. She choked down the fluid, and then gasped for air as Morta and Deviron released their grip. The defeated girl dug her chin into her chest and tried to hold back the tears.

Satisfied that the serum had been administered, Morta stood tall and breathed a triumphant sigh. "Now, it will just take a few minutes to take effect. Deviron will escort you to pick up the little bundle of joy and then you can make your delivery to your new master."

"What about the others?" Deviron asked.

Morta looked slyly at her prisoner. "Kaitlyn can help encourage them to wear the crystals; it will counter the graces that have been protecting them and make it easier to lead them all to The Devourer."

Just then, there was a loud noise outside the chamber.

"You two!" Morta called out to Skullen and Scaylen. "Get out there and see what made that noise. Where is Wicken?"

Deviron grunted, "You told him to guard the entrance to the cavern back at the house. He's still there."

"Good," Morta snapped, "at least we won't have to worry about the brats attempting to rescue the others."

She thought for a moment. "Although, they do have the assistance from the saint. Deviron! Check on the prisoners, I'm going to alert the master. Something doesn't feel right."

She turned her attention to Kaitlyn. "You sit tight. I'll be back shortly and we can get the offering underway." She slipped away. There was something unnerving about the disturbance outside, and she no longer felt confident that everything was under control. She hurried toward a small opening in the wall, which shrouded a darkened staircase, leading down to a lower tunnel. She would approach The Devourer from the lowest balcony in the Black void. She breathed in deeply and prepared herself for the encounter. He always left her feeling anxious and unraveled.

If she had been more settled, perhaps she would have noticed the change in the air, as an invisible saint and his companion swept by her at the entrance of the Chamber of Ansmacht.

Kaitlyn sat listlessly as she sniffed back tears. She was sore and tired and could almost feel the poisonous serum spreading throughout her body. She had never felt so scared and alone.

"It's okay, my dear."

Kaitlyn jumped. "Who's there?" she darted her eyes across the room. "Where are you?"

Pulling back his hood, Padre Pio suddenly appeared. Kaitlyn almost screamed, but the saint quickly and gently pressed his hand to her lips.

"Shhhh! Please," he whispered in earnest, "we don't want to alert Morta or her men."

Kaitlyn was all astonishment. "How did you just appear like that? And aren't you the man who helped fix my car earlier?" She was a picture of confusion.

"We're here to rescue you," the old man replied.

"Wait... we're?" Kaitlyn responded with a puzzled look.

"I'm here too, Kaitlyn." Suddenly Liam popped into view, adjusting his hood.

"Oh wow," Kaitlyn whispered feebly, "how did you... you can make yourself invisible?"

Liam chuckled, "Never mind that, we need to get you out

of here."

Kaitlyn's head fell forward and she started sobbing. "It's too late," she said. "They forced me to drink some kind of possessive potion. I can already feel it taking over. I'm not going to be able to control myself soon. I'll just be their puppet and they'll be using me to deliver baby Callie to their master."

Padre Pio lifted the girl's chin and spoke gently, "Peace, Child; there is always a way. Our Master is the true Master, and if he can make a way in the wilderness, he will make a way for you." He turned to Liam, beckoning him, "Come, lay your hands on your cousin's head and ask for God's blessing."

Liam was confused, but he obeyed the saint. He placed his hands delicately on Kaitlyn's head and began to pray. Kaitlyn jumped, as the contact was almost electric. A warm, tingling surge made its way down from her head, traveling through her neck, into her arms, and through her hands and fingers. She could almost see a flash of sparkling light jolting from her extremities. The current traveled all the way down to her toes, and she was left feeling rejuvenated and joyful.

"It's gone!" she gasped. "I can feel it. It's completely gone!" She glanced around the room. "Can we get out of here now?"

"Of course," Padre Pio replied as he began to loosen the leather straps restraining her hands and feet. But almost as he touched the bindings, a black swirl grew in the ceiling. The flashes of red eyes and the maddening flurry of dark, leathery wings spiraled down toward the unsuspecting visitors.

"Scathes!" St. Pio cried, "Liam, draw your sword!"

Kaitlyn ducked her head as the contorted, bat-like creatures dove toward them. Liam swung his sword, a streak of blue light. The animals screeched and drew back to the ceiling, gaining new momentum. Padre Pio kept working on Kaitlyn's restraints and soon she was free.

"Stay close to the ground, and cover your head," he commanded. "These demonic rodents are full manifestations of evil. They will not give up easily. Liam, stand your ground!"

The creatures swarmed at an even greater speed and became a maniacal, fluttering tornado. Liam stood firm and ready as the beasts drew near. He sliced his weapon through the air, cutting into the funnel. Several of the flying rodents shrieked in pain, hitting the ground and knocking over glass jars and furnishings. The carcasses seemed to fizzle into nothingness.

"Behind you!" St. Pio called out. Liam turned to see the attack coming from behind. He thought it was too late, but just as the creatures were ready to make contact, a vibrant shield flashed into view, zapping several of them and turning them to dust. The bold beasts shot back up to the ceiling, regrouping and preparing for their next attack.

"Can I help?" Kaitlyn called out.

St. Pio smiled assuredly at the girl. "Indeed, you can," he replied warmly. He turned to Liam, beckoning the boy. "Liam, come here and hold out your sword!" Liam lowered himself to the floor where Kaitlyn was taking cover. He extended the glorious weapon toward his cousin.

The children could hear the screeches from the Scathes, growing louder and more frantic.

"Never mind them," the padre asserted. "Kaitlyn, grasp the handle alongside your cousin." Kaitlyn followed the order, as the saint began to speak ever more boldly, "Isaiah 43:19—Forget the former things of the past, see I am about to do a new thing; now it springs forth, do you not perceive it? I will make a way…"

Kaitlyn cut in, excitedly, "In the wilderness!"

Padre Pio looked up at her with a twinkle in his eye, "And so he shall."

Just then the sword flashed with great intensity and seemed to split in two. Both children now each held their own double-edged sword. They jumped to their feet just as the swarming Scathes shot down for their next attack. Liam and Kaitlyn swung their mighty weapons, sending the beasts flying in disjointed circles. They crippled the demonic masses, sending them flying in disjointed, desperate circles.

CHAPTER 24

THE TWO BROTHERS CAREFULLY SURVEYED the area outside of the chamber.

"Over here!" a voice rang out. The men stopped short.

"This way," said Skullen in a dull, drone-like voice.

"Nuh-uh!" another voice echoed in the opposite direction, followed by a shrill of giggles. The two henchmen looked at each other. Through a series of hand motions, they agreed to set off in different directions.

"Little girl?" Scaylen cooed. "Come out, come out, wherever you are... " He slowly entered the West Tunnel. It was a series of stone ripples and archaic sediment. He scanned the area, squinting and peering behind large boulders that were deposited along the path. "Come on, you don't need to be scared."

"BOO!" Angelica yelled. The man jumped, turning in circles, swiping at the air surrounding him.

"WHERE ARE YOU?!" he growled. He was met with another peal of laughter.

"Come and get me!" the small voice teased. "This way, Slow Poke!"

He quickened his pace through the stone corridor and soon entered into the cave.

"Okay," he spat out, his voice echoing off the concave walls, "enough with the games! Where are you?"

"Over here," Angelica said innocently. She had removed her hood and was in plain sight, standing at the opening of the cave. "What's wrong, Mr. Big Guy?" she giggled. "Can't catch one little girl?" Angelica placed her hands defiantly on her hips and dashed out the cave, rounding a sharp corner to the pathway beyond. Once outside, she quickly pulled up her hood and crouched in a tight ball on the ground. She hoped her helmet and breastplate would prove strong and steadfast.

Scaylen had had enough of the taunting. He barreled after the girl, turning the corner full throttle. In a moment of confusion and panic, he tripped over something that felt like a large boulder and found himself flying through the air. He tried to catch himself on the path, but it was steeply sloped and he helplessly slid on his back, down toward the pit. He prepared himself for the huge impending plunge, when all of sudden he jolted to a stop.

PANG! PANG!

Scaylen was dangling off the edge of the cliff. He looked just above both his shoulders and was astonished to find two glowing blue daggers planted deeply through his thick, leather shirt, pinning him to the side of the pit.

Angelica pulled back her hood. Her hair hung over her face as she peered down at the henchman. "You nicked my shoulders!" the man cried out.

"Sorry!" Angelica answered, "I could pull them out... buuut then you'd fall, 'cause I don't think I'm strong enough to hold you up." She shrugged. "Would you like me to lend you my daggers for a little while longer?"

Scaylen helplessly looked up at the girl and blurted out, "Yes!"

Angelica sighed, "Manners?"

Scaylen frowned, but begrudgingly muttered, "Please and thank you." She patted his head and went on her way... .

"Show yourself!" Skullen sneered.

He was dizzy from aimlessly following the echoes of Mary's voice. She was enjoying her game of cat and mouse, baiting the sordid henchman. Her footwear masked even the slightest sound of her movements, and she easily danced past Skullen. It was almost too easy. Emboldened by her supernatural abilities, she passed even closer to him.

Skullen closed his eyes and started to chuckle. "Oh, you have no idea who you're up against, Little Girl," he crooned. "You may be able to hide from my view, but... "

Mary froze, not liking the tone of his voice. Skullen breathed in deeply and smiled, "Strawberries and wildflowers." In one swift motion, he darted toward her, clawing and snaring a fistful of fabric from her cape.

Mary gasped as the cape was wrenched off her shoulders and she realized she was no longer shrouded in invisibility.

"Hello," Skullen said coyly. "You were in the Northern Tunnel, before. I smelled you." He took a step toward her.

"Stay where you are!" Mary called out. "I'm armed!" She pulled out her crossbow and pointed it toward the henchman.

He stopped and surveyed the weapon. "That's an impressive weapon for such a small girl," he said. "I'm willing to bet you have no idea how to use it." He took a step toward her.

"Oh, you really want to try me? Are you feeling LUCKY, Henchman??" Mary was caught up in her greatest performance ever. "ARE YOU?! ARE YOU?! 'Cause just maybe I'm 10 for 10 at hitting my mark! Just maybe you're about to experience the wrath of my crossbow! Are you ready to meet your maker, Henchman?! I'm guessing there's no confessional in this hellish lair, so I'm willing to bet you're not—which means *you* are in big trouble!"

"Umm... " he mustered, "Whoa... "

He slowly backed up holding his hands mid-air in surrender. "Hey, let's just take it easy," he said, in effort to calm the deranged little girl, whose eyes were wild with manic confidence.

"Give me back my cloak!" Mary demanded.

"Sure... here... take it. Just... just stay calm." Skullen fashioned the garment into a tight ball. "Here!" he hollered, suddenly whipping the fabric at her head and knocking Mary back onto the ground. The crossbow flew from her hands and landed about ten feet away. Skullen dove in its direction, slithering and seeking to take control of the illuminated weapon, but as he attempted to grab it, his fingers sank through the object and he found himself merely scratching at the dirt beneath.

"What's going on?" his voice was seething with annoyance, as he continued his attempt at grasping the crossbow. "It's just a hologram! You messing with me, Little Girl??"

"Nope!" Mary replied breathlessly. The weapon rose and floated through the air. She threw her head back, in triumphant laughter. She was firmly holding the crossbow, and pointing it in Skullen's direction. "It's real all right! It's just that it can't be held by someone who doesn't believe in, or respect, God's Word."

Mary looked sympathetically at the henchman. "You're really missing out."

Skullen stood up. He was furious and fed up. He let out an exasperated growl and lurched toward the young girl, but tripped suddenly on a hard, hidden object. He was propelled through the air, knocking his head on the rocky ground. The lair seemed to spin, and in his dizziness, Skullen briefly caught sight of a flash of golden curls popping into view, just before falling over and knocking his head once more.

"Poor guy," Angelica sighed as she stood up, wiping the dust from her knees. "I think he's gonna wake up with a really bad headache."

Mary looked proudly at her little sister, "You're very good at tripping people."

Angelica shrugged modestly. "Hidden talent."

Just then, she fell to the ground. She was being dragged on her belly toward the pit.

"LET GO OF HER!" Mary yelled. She could see the deranged henchman, crawling, snarling, and heaving Angelica. His hand was locked tightly around her leg, as she cried out in protest. Mary lifted her crossbow once more. "I still have my weapon! And I'm *still* not afraid to use it!"

Skullen smiled deviously, "You can't fool me! I'm willing to bet your holographic crossbow shoots holographic arrows, and that's hardly somethin' to worry about."

Mary winced. She didn't really want to shoot anybody, but her sister was in danger.

"You leave me no choice!" she called out.

Skullen stopped, still grasping Angelica's leg. He glared at Mary, almost daring her to take the shot.

Suddenly, something just over Mary's shoulder caught his attention. He froze, eyes wide, and muttered, "We're in trouble."

Mary stared at the henchman, confused and perturbed. She felt a blast of wind from behind her and heard a strange chorus of shrieks. She turned her head just as several large, black creatures brushed against her back. They were pouring out of the Chamber of Ansmacht. She screamed and gripped her crossbow even tighter.

PHIFT!

She fell back and covered her head with her arms as the gust of dark-winged beasts flew over. They dove together in unison, making their way into the pit. Mary waited for the dust to settle. She was certain that, in all the confusion, a shot had been fired from the crossbow. She saw her younger sister, curled up in a ball on the ground.

"Are you okay?" she called out.

"No... ," the voice that answered didn't belong to Angelica. It was deep, raw, and remorseful. "Guess those arrows aren't just holographic after all."

Skullen sat, slumped forward, his hand pressed against his chest.

"I'm so sorry," Mary said softly. "I really didn't mean to... "

Skullen laughed weakly. He pulled his hand away from his chest, lifting it and turning it over. "Huh," he puffed out, "no blood. Strangest thing, 'cause I can sure feel it wedged in my heart." He began to cry loud, heaving, blubbering sobs. It was not the cry of one in pain, but more so, the sound of a tormented little boy, mourning the loss of his most favorite toy in the whole world.

Mary was dumbfounded.

Angelica stood up slowly. "I was not expecting that," she

said, fully stunned. She turned to Skullen, gently placing her hand on his shoulder. "Are you going to be okay?"

Skullen stood up shaking his head and grasping his chest once again. "I dunno," he said, shoulders slumped, trying hard to breathe through the tears. "I think I just need some time alone." He stumbled away, slumped over, weeping uncontrollably.

Mary and Angelica stared at each other in utter disbelief.

"Children!" They turned to see Padre Pio, Liam, and Kaitlyn exiting the Chamber of Ansmacht behind them. The two girls ran and hugged the saint.

"We are sooo glad to see you!" they cried out at once.

Mary looked squarely at the old man, "I shot Skullen in the heart," she said solemnly. "I really didn't mean to... is he going to be all right?"

Padre Pio smiled, assuring the young girl with a gentle pat on the head. "For the first time in his life," he sighed, "he's going to be more than all right."

"But now," the saint continued, "pray for your parents."

Angelica's eyes widened. "Are they here? Are they okay?" she asked.

Padre Pio nodded, "They have entered the lair and are still following instructions, but they've been asked to separate for the time being to attend to varied tasks. Your father will need prayers for great courage and strength. Your mother will be facing Morta, and she requires the charity of your prayers, as she is being called to immense trust and mercy."

"Kaitlyn, I must ask a favor of you," the saint said, turning to the young girl. "If you would be so kind as to lend Angelica your sword for the time being, I think I have a plan that will help tremendously in facing what lies ahead."

Angelica jumped excitedly. "Yes! That would be great!" she almost shouted. "Sorry, it's just that I'm kinda disappointed that Scaylen is still *borrowing* my daggers."

Kaitlyn smiled and willingly handed the sword over to her little cousin. "You can borrow my cape!" the golden haired girl offered in return.

"Cool. Thanks," Kaitlyn laughed.

The Padre's eyes twinkled mischievously. "Once again, this plan may require a dramatic flare."

CHAPTER 25

CHRISTIAN AND ALLORA HAD MADE IT TO THE cage containing their youngest siblings. "Hey, little ones," Allora whispered, as she knelt down beside the door, pressing her face between the bars, "we're here. Everything's going to be okay."

"ALLORA!" the chubby faced little boy ran to meet her.

"Shhhh! Joa, you have to be very quiet," she warned her little brother. "We don't want anyone to hear us."

Joachim nodded solemnly. "Yeah," he said, "'cause they all weally mean." Allora nodded in agreement.

"Oh Allora, I'm so happy you're here," Serena said, joining her brother at the gate. She still had little Callie in her arms. "Can you get us out?"

Christian pulled out his sword. "We're going to try," he whispered. "Just stand back."

The sword glowed, a bluish dazzling hue. Serena and the littles all gasped excitedly. Very carefully, he placed the tip of the blade into the lock securing the door. With a flash of light, the lock easily released its hold and fell to the ground.

Suddenly, Christian felt a strong hand grasp his shoulder. He whirled around, holding his sword out before him.

"Whoa!" said a deep voice. The man he faced was a picture of surprise and joy.

"Dad!" Christian cried out. He threw himself into his father's arms, "I'm so glad to see you! How did you get here?"

Patrick laughed, "Just following instructions, and Instruction #7 says: Hug your children." He paused slightly, "Although, there was no mention of being threatened by a sword in the process."

He looked at his little ones, still shaken from their experience of captivity. He felt terrible that they had had to endure so much. "Come here, all of you," he said gently, beckoning them. He swept Joa up into a bear hug, whispering words of comfort and assuring him that he was safe.

Kiara clamped onto her father's leg. "My stay with you," she peeped.

"Of course," her father replied. He then called to the small twins. "Come on James and Jacinta," he said. James toddled over to his daddy, raising his arms with delight.

"Are you all right, big guy?" Patrick asked the blond one-year-old.

"Humph," he replied (which was his way of saying *yes*).

Jacinta frowned, as if to share her disapproval of the whole ordeal. "Are you okay, Cinta?" Patrick asked softly.

"Eeeewwww!" Jacinta replied (again, her most favorite word). He then wrapped his arms around Serena, who was still holding little Callie. "We're going to get you out of here," he assured them both.

"Christian," Patrick said, turning back to his son, "my next instruction is for you to clear the bridge."

Christian looked confused. "Clear it?" he said. "There's nothing to clear."

"There will be," his father said solemnly. "This was, by far, my most descriptive instruction. It says that The Devourer has now been alerted to your presence and has charged some form of creature, called *Scathes*, to protect the bridge. You'll need your sword to prepare the way for the others. Allora, it says you are to assist in the battle..."

Allora turned around, revealing the large bow and quiver of arrows strapped to her back.

"Wow!" Patrick said, laughing, "I see you're well equipped for the task!"

Allora nodded confidently, but then she turned her head suddenly toward the pit. "I think I hear something," she whispered. She looked at her father, eyes wide with concern. "They're coming."

Patrick could hear it now too: an unfamiliar chorus of screeches, a painfully piercing noise, echoing and growing louder by the second. He ran over to the dark void and could make out what looked like a swarming nest of black, bony wings, alive with sparks of reflective red light. It was rising slowly, nearing the surface. He turned and swiftly scanned the rock wall behind the children. There was an area at the base of the wall that was carved out slightly. He hoped it would serve as a shelter for his small children. "Come on, everyone under there!" he called out as he scooped up the twins and ran toward the shallow trench. The children crouched down and tucked themselves into the crevice, shielded under its rocky lip. Allora pulled out her bow and arrow and stood ready for the imminent attack.

Serena was bent low on her knees, trying to find a space for her and the baby. "Daddy!" she cried out fearfully, "there's no more room under there. Callie and I won't fit; there's nothing to shield us!"

"Yes there is," their father said, and with that he ran to her and held both his daughters, wrapping his body around them, as a human shield. "You'll be safe with me."

Christian grasped his sword. He was shaking, but he comforted himself repeating:

"Even though I walk through the darkest valley, I fear no evil; for You are with me… "

He breathed deeply and raised his sword, awaiting the enemy.

The shrieking creatures shot forth from the depths of darkness: a seemingly endless, black, violent projection to the heights of the lair, where they swirled and gathered momentum before sharply spiraling back down toward the bridge. They were a thick, swarming mass, maniacal and consuming.

Christian held his ground as the dark, rippling hurricane engulfed the bridge. He furrowed his brow. "Clear the bridge?" He whispered under his breath, "Sure, no biggie…" He filled his lungs with air and released a strong, robust war cry.

HAAAAAAAAAAHHHHHH!

Christian bolted into the eye of the storm. His footwear propelled him faster than he expected, but it offered security even on the flimsy wooden panels that made up the floor of the bridge. Once at the center, he wrapped loosened twine dangling from the rails around his wrist and planted himself firmly in place, while using his right arm to wield his sword, cutting into the flurry of flying rodents surrounding him. The bridge swayed and creaked in protest, but Christian continued to strike with all his might. The attack was relentless. Christian swiftly turned in every direction, matching the creatures' speed and vivacity. Every strike was electric in nature, slaying tens of the legion with a single sword pass. A hidden shield surrounded Christian. It appeared briefly, flashing as each unsuspecting creature sought to overcome the boy, zapping them into oblivion.

The Scathes were seething with rage. They flew up to the ceiling once more, their shrieks jumping an octave. The sound penetrated the air like shards of glass scraping the rocky walls. Christian winced at the noise but stood ready for the next attack. The horde of vermin swelled and throbbed, their rotation somehow more focused, more determined. Christian raised his sword once more, as the sordid troop drove down toward the boy. But only a few inches from his blade, they shot out toward Allora. She jumped slightly, but began releasing a slew of arrows into the black mob. Each arrow impaled several of the rodents. They thudded to the ground, then dissipated.

Her shield was vibrant about her, alive with hits and flashes, as the gnarled, winged demons were pulverized in an electric flare. They continued to pour past her, a vicious cyclone. Allora swept the hair from her eyes and turned in horror, as she saw the host heading toward her siblings.

"Christian! Get over here!" she called to her brother. In two swift steps, he was at her side and the two ran toward the creatures. Christian continued striking the beasts with the sword, as Allora filled the air with a flurry of arrows.

Their father was shielding Serena and the baby from the demonic throng. The winged creatures scratched at his back with their sharp, spiny claws, but he seemed oblivious to the impact. Others swept down low, attempting to reach the children who were hidden in the thin crevice, while a large mass of infuriated demons rapped their wings against the rocky wall above, sending down streams of grit and sand. The powdery sediment poured over the lip that was shielding them, as they coughed and huddled more tightly beneath.

Patrick slowly rose, place one hand on Serena's forehead and extended the other toward the littles. He began to utter a prayer. It was long and labored, but the words had a dynamic effect. With each line, ribbons of light appeared, trickling, waving, dancing, and weaving themselves into a tapestry that floated mid-air, and gently blanketed the children. The lustrous spread seemed to harden into a vibrant shield, its presence causing confusion and chaos for the Scathes. They seemed instantly blinded, as though having lost all bearing. Their once powerful shrieks transformed into thin, airy whimpers. They flew in disoriented circles, pathetically and aimlessly flapping their wings. Their numbers were fast shrinking and in their weakened state, Christian and Allora easily vanquished the cruel creatures.

Allora ran over to her father and hugged him tightly. "That was amazing!" she cried out.

"*You two* were amazing!" he replied.

Christian rushed over and asked, "What was that prayer you prayed over the littles?"

His father smiled and said, "A very appropriate prayer: *St. Patrick's Breastplate*."

"Wow!" Allora said delightedly, "Appropriate and powerful!"

Her father called out to the little ones still hiding in the rocky shelter, "Come on, guys. It's time to go. We have to hurry!" He turned to Allora, "Honey, I need you to lead the way. Get them to St. Pio's cavern. Christian, carry your baby sister and help the little ones across the bridge. It's not safe and they'll be scared."

Serena tapped his back, "What can I do to help? Do you need me to shoot the bow and arrow? 'Cause I'd really like to try it out." Patrick bent down smiling, as he placed his hand on the six-year-old's shoulder. "You've already been such a big help, in so many ways. You took care of the little ones and made sure they weren't too scared, and you protected Callie. I'm so proud of you." Serena smiled humbly, as he kissed her forehead. "Now, I think it's time to leave."

"Not so fast!" a voice bellowed out behind them. "As much as I hate to break up this touching family moment, I'm afraid that *no one* will be going *anywhere*!"

CHAPTER 26

PATRICK STOOD UP AND STIFFENED HIS JAW, as he stared at the large, caped man approaching.

"Allora, go now," his voice was steady. He kept his eyes locked on Deviron. The children started across the bridge. They moved along cautiously, from one board to the next, as each panel shifted and the bridge swayed dangerously.

"I repeat: *NO ONE WILL BE GOING ANYWHERE!*" Deviron called out angrily as he quickened his pace. The children hurried along the bridge. The sound of twine snapping made them halt momentarily and grab on more firmly to the braided rails.

"Dad!" Christian called out before stepping onto the bridge. Patrick turned, only for a moment, as Christian tossed his sword in his direction. Patrick made a quick, smooth catch and after slicing the weapon through the air, held it out toward the menacing figure.

"Stay where you are!" he commanded.

Deviron stopped dead in his tracks. "That's a solid piece of metal," he said dryly, "but, I have my orders directly from the master, so there's nothing that's going to stop me from getting those kids."

Patrick stood his ground. "Not happening," he said firmly. "I'm warning you: don't move!"

"Oooh," Deviron sneered, "but you've all made it so easy for me. One big tilt of the bridge, one good shake down, and I can feed the master a mouthful of offerings."

The sound of another piece of twine snapping, and the jolt of the bridge, made all the children cry out. Deviron chuckled maniacally, "Or perhaps the bridge will do all the work for me."

Patrick turned his head to his children. "Keep going!" he called out. Christian echoed his father's command and ushered the children onward. Deviron snarled impatiently and suddenly barreled toward the bridge.

Patrick ordered the villain to stop, but he raged forward. The children gasped and froze in place. Their father lifted his sword, holding fast, as Deviron ran straight at him. The blade speared the gigantic man, and he looked at Patrick in sheer disbelief. Patrick released his grip. Deviron stumbled backward. He frantically grabbed at the sword's majestic handle, now a fixture protruding from his chest, but it was as though he were merely clawing at light.

A sickly green mist rose from the man. He screamed in pain, before lowering his head. His shoulders shook dramatically. It looked like he was convulsing, before he let loose a peal of cruel laughter. He stopped short and raised his eyes to meet his foes'.

"We are nine," he said, his tone fierce, "FAELES!"

A voice called out from behind him, "You *were* nine." It was Padre Pio. "In the name of our dear friends The Angels, I cast out the first wretched demon who has taken hold of this man. Faeles, now you are but eight." Deviron growled at the robed man. Mary and Angelica joined the saint, standing on either side of him.

"Faeles means tomcat," Mary whispered. "Why did he yell that?"

"Nine lives have been living within him," the saint answered, his gaze sternly fixed on Deviron. "We will need to call out each one. As long as the Sword of the Spirit which is the Word of God is embedded in his heart, we will be able to evict the other inhabitants."

Deviron grimaced, as Padre Pio raised his voice. "In the name of the Archangels, I call out the demon who used to belong to your choir. You must go! In the name of the Principalities and Virtues, I call out the third and fourth of the foul creatures ! In the name of the Dominions and Powers, I say to the fifth and sixth who were once a part of those heavenly choirs, you, villainous ones, are no longer welcome here! In the name of the Thrones, you, demon of impatience, I command you to leave this man! And you, the eighth Inhabitant, vile, heinous creature, once a member of the glorious Cherubim, you no longer have power over this man! GO NOW!" Deviron had fallen to his knees. The green mist continued to swirl about him, growing larger with the mention of each new entity. His head was bent and he wailed as the saint continued his enthralling proclamations, "And lastly, in the name of the Seraphim: you who were once given the highest place in heaven, the honor of being closest to the Almighty One, you who chose pride as your god, I now call you out, B... "

"STOP!"

Everyone turned quickly as the cold, callous voice cut through the air. Morta approached, holding a hostage. The children's mother walked slowly in front of her. Morta squeezed her arm with one hand; the other held a large syringe at her prisoner's throat.

"Remove the sword!" Morta called out. "Now! Unless you'd like me to administer the serum."

"LET HER GO!" Patrick cried out, his voice fervent and demanding.

"You heard me," Morta said matter-of-factly. "Remove the sword." Patrick looked to the saint, seeking permission, and was met with a subtle nod. The children's father ran quickly to the slumped man and wrenched the sword out of his chest. He stepped back holding the blade out before him.

MYSTIC INFORMANT **169**

"Now, let her go," he threatened, "or it's going right back in."

Morta eyed him cautiously. She slowly drew the needle away from her hostage's neck. Deviron jumped up, in one violent jerk. He was as an animal having freshly ripped himself from the entanglement of razor-sharp barbed wire. His eyes were wild, crazed with spite.

"STICK HER!" he snarled, stinging with rage, "OR I WILL!"

Patrick raised his sword, ready to defend his bride, when suddenly, the villain cried out in pain. A small glowing shard appeared in his chest. He looked down, stunned.

"Wha... ?" his voice was almost a whisper. As he turned to look behind him, the children saw a large stick protruding from his back. He squinted, making out a short figure standing defiantly on the bridge. Serena held one hand on her hip, and the other clenched Allora's bow. Her lip was tight and her brow fierce.

"LEAVE MY MOTHER ALONE!" she cried out, "YOU BIG BULLY!"

Deviron dropped to his knees. Padre Pio walked over to the man and whispered in his ear, "Beelzebub, depart." He placed his hand gently on Deviron's forehead and blessed him. Deviron lowered his head, wheezing as a green mist seeped from his body, it was pulled into the large, wispy mass still surrounding the brute. The sickening swell, eerie and foul, was promptly siphoned over the edge into the blackened void.

"Eeeewwww!" a little voice called from the bridge. Deviron slumped into a heap, deflated and utterly spent.

Morta didn't miss a beat. She gripped her hostage more tightly and drove the syringe into her throat. Except it didn't break through her skin. The needle's impact was that of a dry, thin twig jabbed into a rock: it readily snapped, as the syringe fell from Morta's fingers, shattering on the ground. The green liquid oozed into the small fissures of the hardened surface underfoot. Morta's eyes were round with fury and confusion.

"What??" she huffed frantically, "I don't understand."

Her hostage turned to face her. She spoke calmly and sympathetically, "I'm wearing 'St. Patrick's Breastplate,' courtesy of my Beloved." She caught her husband's eye and smiled with gratitude. Turning back to her friend, she reached into her pocket and pulled out an envelope. "Morta, this is for you," she said softly, "please take it. It's very important. I think you'll appreciate it."

Morta looked both confused and disgusted. "I don't want anything from you," she spat out. She ripped the envelope from her friend's hand and crumpled it, throwing it to the ground, and as an extra measure of defiance, she stepped on it, grinding her heel in an attempt to shred and defile the gift. Her friend sadly lowered her head.

Morta turned her attention to the children still attempting to cross the bridge. In a shriek of panic, she belted out, "MASTER!"

CHAPTER 27

THE GROUND TREMBLED. THE SOUND OF boulders cracking and rocks catapulting resonated throughout the lair. The bridge began to sway and little voices wailed in protest.

Christian braced himself, holding little Callie close to his chest and wrapping his other arm around the roped rails. He could see waves of light, as graceful hands steadying the small children, protecting and securing them despite the incessant shaking. The tip of what looked like a large boulder rose from the pit, the crowning of an enormous figure. A bulging, stone forehead, a disfigured, animal-like snout, slowly emerged. Three sunken, hollowed out eyes met the crowd of stunned onlookers, as whiffs of red smoke seeped through the stony sockets. A mouth of cruel fangs, and overcrowded eruptions of teeth, glared at them as the brazen jaw became visible. Though but a mountainous idol, the statuesque structure seemed alive, glowing, rising and towering over them. The body was a cave-like furnace, harboring red, intense flames. Heat poured out from a large opening at the belly. It was both oppressive and demanding.

Padre Pio looked urgently toward the bridge. "Dear friends," he called out, "hurry! Get the children to safety!"

The sound of the tired ropes pulling and ripping alerted Christian to a weakened section close to the posts at the entry to the bridge. The twined rails were fastened tightly around the structures but had become severely frayed. They were now breaking apart from the friction caused by the swaying and the added weight of the large group of people (however small in stature) occupying the bridge.

"Dad! The bridge is going to collapse!" Christian cried in earnest. "Help me!"

He ran back to the post and laid Baby Callie on the ground beyond the structure. He fixed his hands on the ropes, offering support for the others. His father was soon at his side, holding the rail extending from the other post.

"HURRY!" Patrick called out to the young children, "Get to the other side!" Christian could see the angelic figures herding the littlest ones across to safety. Finally, Allora, Serena, and the last of the littles were safely on the path headed to the northern tunnel.

"Christian," Patrick said, his voice full of concern, "get the baby and join the children. I'll try to secure both sides of the bridge."

"I don't think the bridge will hold," Christian said hesitantly.

"We have to at least try," his father responded. "We need to get her out of here!" Christian nodded reluctantly, but as he turned to pick up his sister, he realized she was no longer in the place where he had left her.

Panic stricken, he called out to his father, "She's gone!"

"What?!" Patrick called back, releasing his grip on the ropes. The bridge snapped instantly! Panels of wood trickled into the void, as the severed half fluttered down and was left dangling against the far side of the pit. Patrick frowned in dismay, but his focus was on finding his little girl. Christian and his father scanned the area. "We have to find her!" Patrick said urgently. His heart was racing. The presence of The Devourer made Callie's disappearance all the more distressful.

Finally, he spotted her. She was in her cousin Kaitlyn's arms. Kaitlyn was cradling the infant, her eyes fixed on the enormous formation. She was walking slowly in its direction, her face void of all human emotion. She seemed in a daze, yet infused with determination.

"Kaitlyn! What are you doing?!" her aunt cried out, as the girl plowed past her.

Morta's smile was shrewd and pernicious. "She's being compelled to make an offering."

Liam stepped forward, "Kaitlyn, I don't understand! You

were healed! You don't have to do this!"

"Oh, but she does," Morta replied, her tone coarse and unfeeling. "Even the slightest trace of my solution overpowers the senses. You may have tried to heal her, but the tiniest remnant of serum is enough to carry out the mission."

"Kaitlyn, PLEASE!" Mary exclaimed. "She's just a baby! You have to fight this!"

Kaitlyn's eyes flickered like embers, reflecting the deadly red glow surging from the opening as it continued to vibrate and ascend before her. The colossal monstrosity finally came to a scraping halt, wedged between the walls of the pit.

A voice, fully terrifying, raw, and grinding, bellowed from the abominable figure, "I HUNGER! BRING THE INNOCENT TO ME!" All at once, the family members ran toward Kaitlyn, shouting, pleading, and imploring her to turn away from the sacrificial site. Suddenly, the large jaw of the statue dropped open with a loud crank and seemed to breathe in deeply.

Padre Pio gasped. "GET BACK, EVERYONE!" he insisted. The children and their parents heeded the saint's warning and pulled back, just as a ferocious, unrelenting blast of flames poured out from the orifice. The children's shields flickered before them, protecting them from the intense heat. Even Morta was thrown back from the impact of the blast. Kaitlyn was safely inside the perimeter. The force of the flames had been directed just behind her, creating a blazing wall, separating her from the others. She stood before the opening and lifted the child. Callie began to fidget and cry.

"Closer!" the voice commanded.

Morta was sprawled on the ground. She sat up slowly. She was sore and her vision was slightly blurred. She squeezed her eyes closed, before opening them and attempting to focus on her surroundings. A sharp, bright object caught her eye. She looked more closely; it was the envelope that she had crumpled up and cast down. But oddly enough, it was in perfect condition: not a single crease, not the slightest wrinkle, even after her attempt at destroying it. The pristine paper was gleaming, vibrantly white. She couldn't help herself. "How is this possible?" she asked, picking it up with trembling fingers. She opened it slowly, releasing a fragrant aroma.

"Lillies," she whispered, "it can't be... " She pulled out the parchment and could hardly breathe as the words pressed upon her heart:

My Beloved Morta,

I have not abandoned you.

I love you beyond all imagining.

I have been seeking you, and longing to catch your eye, even as you believed you were alone.

It is time for you to return to me.

Three years ago, you believed your actions had permanently stripped you of the title Mother.

You thought after abandoning your little one, she would never want you back.

That was a lie. A lie your enemy still wants you to believe.

The Devourer fed you hopelessness and deception, and it kindled within you self-hatred and regret.

You felt ashamed, broken, and unworthy of anything good in life.

But I am calling you into the light.

Your Lily has never stopped loving you. Even at the tender age of three, she asks about you and prays for the mommy she so desperately wants to know. She would love nothing more than to be held in Your arms.

I would love nothing more than to have you run into mine.

Awake your soul.

Come alive that you may turn your heart to the child who awaits you.

Embrace my mercy, for you are never too far from my love.

Remember: I came, that you might have life, and have it abundantly.

Now live, Dear One. Come back to life.

A warm stream, poured down Morta's cheeks. She was shaken to the core, the grueling pain rising from the pit of her stomach to the back of her throat. She hunched over, wailing. She closed her eyes and could almost see the small figure reaching out her arms. For the first time ever, she could feel the claws digging into her shoulders, holding her back.

"Let me GO!" she cried out. She turned to see Padre Pio walking toward her. "What do I do?" she exclaimed. "I thought it was too late for me! I want to change! Can I truly be free?"

He bent down and looked sympathetically at the woman. Sections of her black hair were plastered on her face from the tears and grit.

"If the One True Lord sets you free," he said, looking deep within her, speaking to her very soul, "you will be free indeed." He blessed her and then turned his attention to the two figures holding her captive. "This obsession has been terminated. You no longer have power over her. Release your grip!"

The dark beings protested, but were aware of their imminent defeat. They fizzled out as Morta felt the weight lift from her shoulders. Padre Pio spoke gently to the penitent woman, "Ask your angel to come back to you. He has been waiting all this time at a distance, but will return the moment you extend the invitation." He grew very serious. "Your journey now will be quite difficult. You will have to work hard to change your life completely, and it will be more trying than you could ever imagine, but there is great hope for you, and there is one who is now ready to be united with... her mother."

Morta smiled. "Yes, my Lily. And I'd do anything to be able to hold her in my arms... anything."

"Make use of the Sacrament of Confession," the saint instructed. "Your new life will begin there."

"PADRE PIO!" the children's mother cried out to the saint, her eyes streaming with tears. "How can we rescue *my* baby?"

The saint approached her and spoke calmly, "Trust, Daughter." She nodded, even though she felt her heart splintering.

The Devourer continued to urge Kaitlyn to draw near. "Feed the child to the flame," he whispered. For centuries children had been laid at his feet, even at the hands of their own parents, but his appetite was insatiable. He stared intently at the infant. The bearer carefully brought the baby back toward her chest and then quickly pulled up the hood of her cape.

Suddenly, she was gone.

He roared, the sound causing the entire lair to vibrate. Pieces of rock fell from the ceiling, and more cracks and lesions appeared in the surfaces. "WHERE ARE YOU???!"

Angelica peered through the flames. She could see soft footprints forming as the invisible teenager bolted around the side of the statue. The mass of rock had created a perfect bridge, allowing Kaitlyn to cross safely to the other side with little Callie. She watched as the footprints revealed her cousin had finally made it to the Northern Tunnel, well on her way to St. Pio's cavern. She breathed an immense sigh of relief and smiled at Mary.

"They made it!" she exclaimed.

Mary beamed, "I knew she could do it!"

"Now I think we should get out of here too," Liam said,

joining them.

The saint raised his hand to the wall of fire, soothing the torrential flames. He walked toward the odious structure and called forth in a bold, unfaltering voice, "You have failed!"

The Devourer chuckled, brewing in his loathsome arrogance. "I have NOT!" he declared, "You are all still in MY LAIR! These children whom you've sought to protect are in MY DOMAIN!"

Padre Pio snorted, which made Angelica giggle in spite of the menacing presence. "You have always relied on humans to feed you: the confused, the selfish, the broken, and the ignorant. You have preyed on their fears and filled their minds with deceit. You have convinced them to sacrifice their children and, in turn, fed them empty promises. But now, you are alone. Where are your followers? You sought to break apart this family, and instead, they've broken through the lies that kept your despondent servants in a state of slavery. You tried to smother their light, and instead they have pierced through your darkness. We will now be taking our leave and you, pathetic, depraved fossil of a beast, will remain hungry." His words were as spears, driven steadily into the villain's pregnant ego. "There is no one here to feed you now. You are alone: abandoned and powerless."

Viciously enraged, the detestable being opened his jaw once more, threatening to blast those before him. Padre Pio spoke out, "I think you are well aware that the heavenly host assigned to protect your former followers are present and now fully activated."

Pools of light appeared suddenly, swirling and growing. They seemed to stretch to the heights of the lair, forming a brilliant wall between The Devourer and the group of awestruck spectators. It was an astoundingly beautiful sight: a rippling, luminescent cascade.

Morta joined the saint, standing firm and resolute. "You LIED to me!" she called out to the demon, "I am no longer your prisoner!"

Deviron followed behind. Still sluggish, he leaned on Patrick, who used all his strength to support the gigantic man. Skullen had reemerged too, joining the group. He was accompanied by Scaylen, freshly rescued and released with the help of Christian (who had excitedly pocketed Angelica's daggers).

They all walked on, past the stone structure, toward the Northern Tunnel. The foul demon's rage erupted. The entire lair shook, as the spurned creature became consumed with fury. The group dodged broken fragments of rock falling and smashing on the path before them.

"Hurry!" the saint urged. The group made their way through a blanket of dust and debris, swiftly escaping into the tunnel, as the large, bouldered monument capsized, crumbling into the pit. Black smoke billowed into the tunnel behind the saint and his companions as they made their way to the red door.

They all breathed a sigh of relief. Deviron was still being propped up by Patrick.

"Sorry 'bout all of that," he muttered sheepishly.

Patrick readily forgave the large man but then gave him a questioning look, "Where did you park my van?"

Padre Pio was at the door. He held it open, motioning the group inside. "Come now," he said. He pulled Patrick aside, saying, "Take the second door on your right to get to your van and take the former henchmen with you."

Once everyone was through the red door, the saint peered down the tunnel and breathed a deep sigh of relief. He declared solemnly, "So, my old foe, once again you see how the raging storms you perpetuate only lead to the greater glory of God. He has used this attack to unite their hearts evermore closely to his. I'm sure it brings you no pleasure to realize that this has been for their merit and for the good of many souls." A flash of crimson red sparked within the blackened cloud. The saint stared intently and resolutely before firmly closing the door.

CHAPTER 28

WICKEN HAD FALLEN ASLEEP ON THE grass, just outside the great doors. He woke to the feeling of something sharp poking into his ear.

"Eeeewwww!" a little voice said. He opened his eyes and found himself staring into the big, disapproving hazel eyes of the pint-sized twin. She looked at her fingernail in dismay.

He jumped up. "Whaa?" he murmured. "Did you just put your finger in my ear??"

"Jacinta!" Serena called out. "Leave the poor guy alone... and wash your hands."

Wicken was beside himself. *"Poor guy*? What is going on??"

Morta suddenly emerged, breathing in the fresh air and reaching up toward the sunlight. "Oh Wicken," she laughed, "you have no idea!"

Allora followed behind. She was still adorned in her

cloak and heavenly armor, but as soon as she rose out of the cavern, all seemed to disappear, as though absorbed into the light of day. She looked down disappointedly. "Awww!" she sighed. "Too bad."

The sound of an engine revving caught everyone's attention. The family's large van pulled up beside the house. Wicken's jaw dropped open as he saw Deviron jump out of the side door, followed by Skullen and Scaylen. The driver, Patrick, rounded the vehicle and extended his hand to Deviron, who readily bypassed the handshake for a big sloppy, emotional hug.

"I'm so confused," Wicken said shaking his head. "What about the master?"

Morta's face became intent and serious. "He's not my master, nor should he be yours," she said. "He's a lying, selfish, weakling, who no longer dominates us. We're free."

Padre Pio ascended the spiral staircase and looked squarely at the stunned henchman. "Hello, Wicken," he said gently, "would you like me to bless you?" Wicken froze but managed a slight nod. Padre Pio closed his eyes and placed his hand over Wicken, praying fervently. Wicken's face became a series of emotions: first fear, then surprise, awe, and wonder, followed by earnest tears.

"Poor guy!" Joa exclaimed, "I think Old Obi-Wan just used his *Jedi mind tricks!*"

The other family members in the cavern emerged. Those who had been adorned in armor saw the luminescent attire evaporate like the morning dew. "It was nice while it lasted," Angelica sighed. They were soon joined by the occupants of the van.

Another vehicle pulled up too, and Kaitlyn's brothers called out from the windows. Michael shouted from the driver's seat, "Kaitlyn, where have you been? You were supposed to have brought the kids to our place! Mom's been so worried about you!"

Kaitlyn handed the baby over to Allora before giving everyone a tight hug. One of the other brothers, Joseph, called out, "Kaitlyn, stop being all mushy, and get over here!"

"You have no idea what we've just been through!" she called back.

Daniel, yelled in reply, "Yes we do! My arms are still sore from lifting Joa up to the monkey bars!!!"

Kaitlyn shook her head and then headed off to the impatient crew. She turned and waved to Padre Pio, calling out, "Thank you!"

"Dear St. Pio, will you stay with us?" Mary asked the saint, "I never want you to go." Padre Pio shook his head and said, "My time with you has come to an end, but as you well know, I will be with you in spirit, praying for your family, and, someday, I also hope to greet you at the eternal gates."

He turned to Morta. "I bet you're eager to be reunited with your little one."

Her eyes were brimming with tears. "Yes," she whispered in earnest.

"Go now, and cling to the sacraments. Look after your friends. You will need to support each other... especially Deviron." He winked teasingly at the large man, who shrugged his shoulders sheepishly. "When you are ready, your Lily will be waiting for you. Although your sister has done well caring for her these past few years, your daughter will be so overjoyed to finally be reunited with her mother. Our Lord will lead you to her very soon. He will make a way for you." Morta was beaming with joy. She turned and hugged each family member, and asked their forgiveness before taking her leave, joined by the four former henchmen.

The children embraced their dear saint, their eyes warm with tears.

"Pray for us," their mother whispered, as she was held close.

"Always," the saint whispered back. He turned his attention to the children. "Remember to say your prayers daily, especially the Rosary, and frequent the sacraments often," he said. "Oh, and remember the incredible power of those little acts of kindness and everyday offerings... as a friend of mine (a dear Spanish priest) has said: *when a Christian carries out with love the most insignificant everyday action, that action overflows with the transcendence of God.* You were blessed in that you were given the gift of *seeing* the reality of the extraordinary graces that came from those seemingly small offerings and sacrifices—most do not. Never forget this experience."

"Can I play in your cavern?" Joa asked Padre Pio.

The saint bent his knee and and placed his hand on the boy's shoulder. "I'm afraid not, little one," he said, standing up and addressing Allora, "May I have the key?"

Allora reached into her pocket and pulled out the object that had begun their adventures. The saint took the key, and cautioning the family to stand back, he raised his hand over the doors. The two grand panels slowly rose, closing, coming together with a flash of light. A great streak of lightning passed along the seam, welding the fissure. Padre Pio placed the key into the keyhole and turned it halfway around. Then something amazing happened. While still inserted, the key began to change shape. The beautiful piece seemed to unravel and twist until it was altogether a different key. The saint removed it promptly, displaying it before the others.

Allora reached out her hand. But the saint shook his head and said, "This is a *new* key, created for a *new* adventure. It will come to you exactly when you need it." He closed his hand tightly around the ornate object, and when he opened it, the key was gone.

"Wow," Angelica breathed softly.

Liam adjusted his glasses, as he pondered aloud, "What about the door in the alley? Will it also be assigned a new key?"

"No," the saint replied, "that door no longer exists. By God's grace, Morta has severed the tie."

He then turned to the sweet faces, ripe with emotion. He blessed each of them and then said softly, "Ciao, my dear, dear children." The parting was swift. One moment he was there and the next, gone.

"That meant '*bye*'," Mary blurted, fighting back tears. "I don't even need my gift to translate that." Liam sighed, only slightly annoyed.

Christian ran to the panels. He knew there was no point in attempting to open the great door. "Do you think we should cover these up or something?" he asked.

His father joined him. "I think we should let Joa have his sandbox back," he said. "We don't know when you'll be called to your next adventure, so until then, let's play."

"YES!" cried Joa. "I'm going to hug my sand!"

"Eeeewwww!" cried someone else.

BEYOND FICTION: SAINT FACTS

BY LIAM DOUGLAS

PADRE PIO WAS BORN ON MAY 25, 1887 IN Pietrelcina, Campania, which is in southern Italy. His parents were poor farmers who were very devout Catholics. They named their son Francesco Forgione. Francesco was given the name Pio (meaning "Pius" in Italian) when he joined the Order of Friars Minor Capuchin. "Padre" means "Father." Padre Pio died in 1968. His feast day is September 23.

Here are 10 facts about Padre Pio:

1. He was so certain that God was calling him to the priesthood, even at the age of five. Because of this, he was very pious and even made offerings and acts of penance, like sleeping on a stone at night.
2. He received the stigmata, sores resembling the wounds of the crucified Jesus. Not only that, but the wounds smelled sweet like roses. Doctors were astounded by how the wounds in his hands were perfectly round.

3. It's true that Padre Pio has a partially incorrupt body. He died in 1968, but to this day he looks as if he's simply sleeping which has amazed many scientists. His body is displayed in a casket made of glass.
4. He was visited by a young priest named Fr. Karol Wojtyla and predicted that he would be elevated one day to "the highest post in the church...". This priest later in life became Pope John Paul II.
5. Padre Pio saw Jesus, Mary, and many angels (including his guardian angel) when he was a child. They continued to appear to him throughout his life.
6. He was known for spending amazingly long periods of time hearing confessions. He would know if someone confessing their sins was intentionally hiding any mortal sins.
7. He is the patron saint of stress relief and adolescents.
8. Padre Pio was able to bilocate, meaning he could be in two places at the same time when he needed to be.
9. He often talked to angels throughout his life, and even told his spiritual children to send their guardian angels to him if they needed his prayers or assistance.
10. Padre Pio had a VERY strong devotion to Our Lady. He loved the rosary and encouraged everyone to pray it daily. He said: *"The Rosary is the weapon given us by Mary to use against the tricks of the infernal enemy."*